Introduction

A SEQUEL TO *MANSFIELD PARK?* WHAT PRESUMPTION! NO, NOT presumption. Love and admiration. *No one* could presume to make any attempt to fill the gap left by Jane Austen. And I have not done so. But, finding myself filled with an overmastering wish to find out what happened after Fanny married Edmund, and when Susan came to live at Mansfield, I had no recourse but to try and work it out by a mixture of imagination and common sense.

—Joan Aiken

Chapter 1

THE SUDDEN AND UNEXPECTED DEATH OF SIR THOMAS BERTRAM, while abroad engaged on business relating to his various properties in the West Indies, could be a cause of nothing but sorrow, dismay, and consternation to the baronet's friends in England. A just administrator, an affectionate parent, a devoted husband, and respected neighbour in the county of Northamptonshire where he resided, Sir Thomas must be missed sincerely by all; yet his nearest family were left in particular and extreme distress, since in so many matters his word had been accepted as final authority; without its head, his household hardly knew how to go on, or how to resolve the innumerable difficulties and perplexities which his loss had occasioned, yet which only he it seemed could resolve.

In the first place it was immediately necessary that one of the baronet's two surviving sons should proceed without delay to Antigua, to settle the numerous matters of business there left in a state of uncompletion by his demise; yet, which son could be spared?

"I cannot part with Tom," lamented his mother, the disconsolate widow. "That Tom should go is wholly out of the question. No, no, I cannot spare Tom.—Yet how can I manage without Edmund?"

As the heir and elder son, it was unquestionably part of the new Sir Thomas's duty to undertake the journey, and so he properly felt himself; but, on the other hand, he could hardly flout his bereaved and sorrowing mother's wishes in the matter. A further consideration, lending additional weight on this side of the question, was the fact that Tom, not four years since, had been so critically ill of a neglected fever that, for some weeks, his life had been despaired of; and, even after amelioration had commenced there had, for a considerable period, been much grave cause for anxiety, since a number of hectic symptoms pointed to a morbid condition of the lungs. These fears had, fortunately, proved to have been misplaced, yet a certain weakness, remaining for several years thereafter, rendered a prolonged sojourn in a tropical climate so unwise that Sir Thomas, although he would have been glad of his elder son's company on the voyage so that Tom might become familiar with the state of his affairs in Antigua, had nevertheless decided against taking him.

"Supposing that Tom should contract the fever a second time, and die in that dreadful place?" wailed Lady Bertram. "No, no, it is not to be thought of. But yet, how shall I ever do without Edmund?"

"My dear ma'am, I am positive that you can manage without Edmund very well," cried the Honourable Mrs. Yates, who had come to lend her voice to the family council.

Miss Julia Bertram, having been so ill-judged as to marry the younger son of a peer, had soon, on becoming more closely acquainted with the limited extent of her husband's fortune, decided to quit the doubtful pleasures of life in London on a straitened income, and console herself by becoming queen of a smaller society. She had persuaded her husband, the Honourable John Yates, to purchase a respectable property in Northamptonshire, not too far distant from Mansfield Park, therefore able to be illumined by some of its lustre. Since then, by almost daily visits to Mansfield, and by longer visits amounting to several months during the course of the year, Mrs. Yates was able to reduce materially her own domestic expenditure, and exert almost as much influence as she wished in Mansfield affairs. Her husband generally found himself very well content to remain at home on these occasions, shooting his coverts, fishing, or hunting six days a week as the season dictated; these, with billiards, were his only occupations.

"But Julia, how shall we ever do without Edmund on Sundays to preach the sermon?" demanded Lady Bertram.

"Do not concern yourself on that head, ma'am!" Edmund, the younger son, had, indeed, long ago settled the necessities of this matter in his own mind. As incumbent of the parish of Mansfield there devolved on him many duties from which he could ill be spared; yet nevertheless he had seen from the first that he must be the one to travel to Antigua. Fixed in this resolution he had already enlisted the aid of an acquaintance in Holy Orders some years older than himself, who, having recovered from a fever contracted during missionary work abroad, had been recommended by his Bishop to take six months' respite in a healthy country parish before returning overseas.

Mr. Wadham had by letter expressed himself happy to oversee the cure of Mansfield and its outlying farms, the matter had been settled, and the gentleman was expected to arrive at the Parsonage shortly.

"I am persuaded, ma'am," continued Edmund Bertram with half a smile, "that you will find my friend Frank Wadham's sermons a decided improvement on mine. He is of a most unimpeachable character, well-bred and amiable, a distinguished preacher, and a devout Christian. I am sure that he will fill my place very well."

"If you say so, Edmund—" replied his mother, sounding only half convinced. And his cousin Susan here asked bluntly,

"But if you go, Edmund—and Mr. Wadham comes to the Parsonage—what about Fanny? What becomes of Fanny?"

Fanny was Edmund's wife. Her sister Susan had, four years ago, at the time of her cousin Tom's illness, been invited to make her home at Mansfield Park, as help, auxiliary, and general comfort to her aunt Bertram. Aged fourteen at that date, and coming from a home which superfluity of children, poor governance, and straitened means had rendered slatternly, turbulent and uncomfortable, Susan had rapidly accustomed herself to the dignities and amenities of Mansfield. Well endowed with quickness of understanding, pleasure in being useful, no inconsiderable force of character, and a disposition to be happy, she had soon become essential to her aunt's comfort, and in a very short time had established herself as the linchpin of the household. Fanny, Susan's more delicately formed and tender elder sister who previously lived at Mansfield, had, at that time, married her cousin Edmund and was now established with her husband at the nearby Parsonage, where their marriage had been blessed first with a remarkably pretty little girl, the apple of her father's eye, and, more recently, with a baby boy.

"Fanny insists on accompanying me," said Edmund.

All the ladies cried out at this.

"Impossible! Not to be thought of! In that hot climate! With her delicate disposition! It would be utter folly—utter madness!"

"You know Fanny, my dear ma'am," said Edmund. "Once she has taken her resolution on a thing, she is not to be swayed. And to tell the truth I shall be exceedingly glad of her company. Fanny thinks justly on all topics, and has a good head on her shoulders for business."

"But Edmund," objected Edmund's older brother, "Fanny is such a puny little thing—so easily fatigued. Walking half a mile knocks her up. She will be prostrated, quite done up, after six weeks in that climate!"

Tom felt not a little ashamed, now the matter had been resolved without his having to put himself out, that *his* being spared the inconvenience and exertion of a journey should occasion his brother's wife being thus laid at risk. Not ill-disposed to his cousin Fanny—he thought her a very good sort of dull little thing—Tom wished her no harm in the world, "*I* have been to Antigua," he continued. "I know what the climate is like. It will not do at all for Fanny. No, no, I will tell you what will be best. She must come up to this house with the children while you are gone, Edmund. She can stay at Mansfield and be looked after. She will be company for my mother."

"Yes, that will be better," agreed his sister Julia. "The children may have the little white attic where Fanny herself used to sleep, and she can be in the East Room; there she will feel quite at home and be no trouble to any body."

A certain curl of the lip betrayed her cousin Susan's sentiments at this arbitrary disposal of Fanny, but Edmund repeated quietly,

"Fanny travels with me, and little William also. That is all decided. If you, ma'am, will be so good as to receive my daughter Mary at Mansfield—"

"The little dear. Of course we shall be happy to have her," sighed Lady Bertram, anticipating no inconvenience to herself in this arrangement, as indeed there would not be, for she could be quite certain that three-year-old Mary would be devotedly cared for by her aunt Susan.

These matters established to everybody's satisfaction, the two brothers went away for a last talk about estate affairs, since, in fact, for the last few months, during Sir Thomas's absence, Edmund the younger brother had been dealing with the greater part of these, while Tom spent time in London and Bath, paid visits to acquaintances, and improved his knowledge of Brighton and Harrowgate. Pasturage, turnips, gamekeepers, which coverts must be attended to, which tenants indulged, which scolded, and which hunters put out to grass, must all be discussed, since Edmund and his wife would be setting sail from Liverpool in two days' time.

"If you will not mind excusing me, Aunt Bertram, while my cousin Julia remains with you," said Susan, "I think I will just run over to the Parsonage to ask my sister about little Mary's clothes, and find out if I can help in any way with her packing."

"Do, my love; go by all means; and tell Fanny that while she is in the West Indies she may as well bring me back a fringed shawl; or, no, perhaps two shawls would be better.'

"Certainly, Aunt."

"That girl does not improve," said Julia, when Susan had left the room. "There is something about her—a certain freedom of manner, a lack of proper modesty, a wish to put herself forward—I have often observed it; she chooses to go her own way without any of that decorum and propriety which you, ma'am, and our dear aunt Norris were so careful to instil into Maria and me. I suppose one cannot hope for anything better—coming from such a very vulgar background as she does—yet after four years amid the elegancies and refinements of Mansfield, one might have expected to see more signs of gentility. It is impossible to be comfortable in her society. And how she grows! She must be more than a head taller than poor

Maria, who was accounted one of the finest young ladies in the country. I confess I cannot admire her looks—she is so high-coloured and coarse. And her eyes! Instead of casting them down demurely as a young lady should who is not out, she stares you straight in the face—it is almost brazen! One is put quite out of countenance. There is no delicacy, no wish to avoid notice. If she went into society she would be giving offence every minute."

"Then," said Lady Bertram calmly, "it is fortunate that Susan does not go into society. Her ways suit *me* well enough—we go on very comfortably together, for she is an active, good-hearted girl, never too tired to untangle my work or take out Pug for an airing. And she has a fine, clear speaking voice; I can hear it plainly when she reads to me, whereas you, Julia, always mumble, and so does Tom."

"I do not consider that she need dress as fine as she does. It is making herself needlessly conspicuous. That gown she had on was by far too bright. And the pattern too large; it does not suit her."

"Her cousin Edmund gave it her, for her birthday."

"Oh—! That was very good in Edmund. He does not remember little Johnny and little Tommy on *their* birthdays," said Mrs. Yates, conveniently forgetting that she herself took no pains to mark the anniversaries of her brother's children. "And then there is something altogether too easy and confident in her way of talking—as if she felt herself quite *on a footing* with the rest of us. Do not you think so, ma'am?"

"Well," said Lady Bertram, after many minutes' slow consideration, "I suppose she is on a footing. Sir Thomas had a decided respect for her mind; he was used to say that she had a remarkable intelligence."

"No doubt my father intended to show indulgence to her, because of where she came from. He made allowances."

"I do not believe so. I have heard Sir Thomas say that if she had been a boy she would have had a good head for politics and should go into Parliament."

"A fine notion!" said Julia with an angry laugh. "Mr. Yates would hardly agree with my father there. I have heard him compare my cousin Susan to a *squawking jay.* He does not at all admire her."

"That is because she corrected him on a point about the slave-trade." said Lady Bertram placidly. "I remember that he was very put out at the time."

"Mamma, I have been thinking," said Mrs. Yates, drawing her chair a little closer to the sopha on which Lady Bertram reclined. "Now that my father has died, do you not think there is a certain impropriety in my cousin Susan remaining under this roof? The household at Mansfield now so very much diminished, just the three of you, my brother Tom, and Susan, and yourself—mischief can come of such a small, close society. Tom and Susan will be in one another's company more than is prudent."

"But you know, my love," pointed out her mother, "that Fanny and Edmund are here every day with the children. And how many times a week are you not coming over from Shawcross with little Johnny and little Tommy.—Where are the little angels, by the bye?"

"I left them over at the Parsonage with Fanny. They quite doat on little Mary and the baby. But, Mamma, I wish you will be thinking seriously about this matter. Susan has remained at Mansfield quite long enough; in my opinion quite long enough. She has derived untold benefits—untold advantages from her residence here. But it is time she went home to Portsmouth. My aunt Price must need her. And she would, I daresay, soon find herself a husband among the dockyard officials or naval officers there. I do not think it wise that she and Tom should be so much thrown into one another's society as they are certain to be from now on."

"But Tom has never paid any especial attention to Susan," said Lady Bertram, after more thought. "It is rather the reverse. He was used to laugh at her when she first came, when she was fourteen, because she spoke rather quick, and had some little expressions that were not quite ladylike; she must have picked them up from her brothers, you know. But since those days he has hardly noticed her; he is become accustomed to her as one of the household."

"But he has been very much away from home these past few months. Now that he is to be more at home—"

"I do not think," pursued Lady Bertram, "that Susan's mother would wish her back in Portsmouth now that the family are moved to a smaller house. My sister Price has never expressed any wish for Susan to return. And besides, I could not spare her. I am sure I could not get on without her."

"But, Mamma, either I or Fanny can very readily perform for you all those small services that you receive at Susan's hands. And Tom, you know, will be marrying soon; it is high time that he did so. And after that his wife will be here to keep you company and Susan will not be needed."

"Married?" repeated her ladyship slowly, as if this idea were a novelty. "Tom, married? Has he shown any signs of partiality to any young lady? I have not been aware of it myself."

"No, Mamma, but then you never go into society. You do not pay visits or receive company or attend balls; you do not see the young ladies that Tom distinguishes with his attentions."

"Does he distinguish young ladies? If that is so," remarked Lady

Bertram after more thought, "then I do not see that you need have any anxieties about his fixing his regard upon Susan."

"Well—Tom is too well-bred for any unsuitable particularity, of course," said his sister quickly, "but I *have* noticed that he has shown a decided interest in Miss Yates. He has danced with her a great number of times at the Northampton Assemblies."

Miss Charlotte Yates was the younger sister of Julia's husband. She now resided with her brother and his wife. A tolerably pretty young lady with very fine teeth, she possessed a decided notion of her own consequence as the youngest daughter of an earl. To display the fine teeth she laughed a great deal, thereby endowing herself with a reputation for wit and gaiety; and the notion of her consequence was of more advantage to her, as she possessed very little else, her impoverished parent having, at his death, left his five daughters with no more than a thousand pounds apiece. Two of her elder sisters had succeeded in securing husbands, two more were, as their brother John put it, "like two old fowls roosting up on the top shelf out of sight."

At twenty-one Charlotte Yates was still sufficiently young to have no real fear that the stigma *old maid* need be applied to her, but she was beginning to think matrimony a duty that should no longer be postponed, and in this opinion her sister-in-law entirely concurred. It had become an object with Julia to find a husband for Charlotte and see her set up her own establishment.

"Indeed—does Tom interest himself in Miss Yates?" asked Lady Bertram in her languid tone. "I was not aware of that. But—now I come to think—somebody—I forget who—told me that Tom had rather distinguished that fair young lady who is a cousin of the Maddoxes over at Stoke—I daresay you know the lady I mean, I do not at this present recall her name.'

"You mean Miss Louisa Harley I suppose? I cannot say that I have ever discerned any sign of *that*. And I am just as glad of it, for Miss Harley—I will not say precisely that she is vulgar, for the Maddoxes are perfectly well connected, but her conversation lacks that elegancy of form that you and I, ma'am, are accustomed to at Mansfield. Whereas our dear Charlotte is a most unexceptionable, nice-spoken, well-bred young lady."

"Yes, Harley. Louisa Harley—that was her name. She had golden hair and sang 'Early One Morning' very sweetly. Now you recall her name to me I remember Tom speaking of her more than once; he said she was a remarkably pretty young lady with a great number of accomplishments."

"Oh, I daresay." cried Mrs. Yates vexedly. "Tom considers any girl *accomplished* if she can sing a couple of ballads, accompany herself on the pianoforte, and understand a charade if it is explained to her. I cannot say that I admire the young lady myself. I believe she would make a decidedly inferior addition to our circle at Mansfield."

"Then," said Lady Bertram tranquilly, "it is fortunate that you say you have observed no sign of Tom's having singled her out in any way. We need have no apprehension on that score. But, in any case, I see no necessity for Tom to marry at present; indeed, not for some time. He is but thirty. He has not spoken to me of marriage. In my opinion we go on very well as we are. I do not care for a change. It is fatiguing to be obliged to converse with some unfamiliar person who does not fully understand one's ways. For my part I think it best that Tom does not marry for at least ten years; there is no occasion in the world for him to be in a hurry. I am sure Sir Thomas would not have wished it. Sir Thomas did not care for hastily made connections."

"When Sir Thomas was *alive,* ma'am, those arguments might

have held force. But now that my poor father is no more, it does seem to me that Tom's marriage is an event greatly to be desired. Now that *he* is Sir Thomas, master of Mansfield Park, one of the most eligible properties in the country, and of such a handsome competence, I do think it of great importance that he should settle down, detach himself from some of his less desirable connections, and in general commence to lead a more regular, more sober life. Mr. Yates entirely agrees as to the propriety of this; he has spoken his views to me on the matter many times."

"Perhaps it would be better if he spoke them to Tom."

"Oh—! Tom takes no heed of what anybody says to him. He never did, you know; he would *listen* to my father's admonitions with a downcast, hangdog, shamefaced look, but I do not recall a single instance of his ever *acting* upon them."

"But he and Mr. Yates are great friends, are they not? It was through Tom that Mr. Yates first came to Mansfield."

"Mr. Yates has changed his tastes since then," replied Julia, not best pleased to be reminded of the period when her husband and her brother had been companions and vied with one another in gambling, card-playing, and race-going. "John and my brother no longer take such pleasure in one another's company."

"Well," said Lady Bertram with a sigh, "perhaps there is something in what you say; perhaps a wife would help to settle Tom. It would not be right, indeed, that he should dissipate the fortune his father amassed with such care."

"Just so, ma'am; and a sensible, practical wife such as my dear Charlotte would be the very person to see *that* did not happen."

"How fortunate it is," pursued Lady Bertram without attending to this, "that it is not of the least consequence *which* among these young ladies Tom decides to bring home as a wife. It can make no difference. The one he chooses will be sure to be ladylike and conformable. And her degree of fortune, or lack of it, need not be a consideration, you know, for Tom is sure to be comfortably provided for, as soon as Edmund has settled the business in Antigua. How fortunate that we need not be troubling ourselves in the matter.—I hope that Susan soon returns from the Parsonage, for my fringe has got into a dreadful tangle; she will have to undo it."

At this moment, indeed, the shouts of little Johnny and little Tommy were to be heard in the hall outside; their cousin Susan had kindly brought them away from the Parsonage, where they had been making their presence felt by teasing their younger cousins, spilling the ink, and pulling the cat's tail.

"Do not bring the little angels in here, Susan," called Lady Bertram, raising her voice very slightly above its accustomed soft monotone, "for their shouting hurts my ears, and besides, they frighten Pug. Give my love to Mr. Yates, Julia, when you return home, and be so good as to tell Christopher Jackson, on your way through the village, that he is to bring his tools up to the servants' hall tomorrow where Mrs. Whittemore has some orders for him."

Thus hinted away, Julia had nothing for it but to summon her little angels to her side and leave, which she did with the usual feelings of irritation resulting from her fruitless efforts to make Lady Bertram take action in the matter of persuading Tom to propose to Miss Yates; or indeed to take any action at all of any kind.

Susan came quickly into the room, looking a trifle put about and discomposed—she had stept into the housekeeper's room on her way back and been obliged there to settle various grievances resulting from a visitation by Mrs. Yates, who seldom failed, on her calls at Mansfield, to have what she called "a comfortable coze with my dear old Whittemore"—which frequently resulted in that lady's giving in her notice and having to be cajoled out of her annoyance by generous doses of sympathy, flattery, and conciliation.

"I do not know why *that one* should think it needful to tell me she saw one of the girls in the village with a flower in her hat; if *Lady Bertram* has no complaint as to my management of the servants—"

"My dear ma'am, you know very well that Lady Bertram thinks, and so does Master Tom, that you manage the house-hold to perfection. If *they* have no fault to find, why should you trouble your head? I believe it is just that Mrs. Yates feels—feels regret for the past, for the old days when she lived here as a girl.'

"I do not recall that she ever took the least interest in house-keeping affairs, or paid any visits to my room in *those* days."

"But *now,* ma'am, you see, she appreciates far more justly the niceties and difficulties of such matters."

Susan reflected, as she said this, that, besides a sheer love of meddling for its own sake in Julia, such a view of the matter was very likely true: brought up amid the sufficiencies and comforts of Mansfield, *Julia Bertram* had yet to learn the anxieties of the Honourable *Mrs. Yates,* endeavouring to appear serenely beforehand with the world on a very inadequate income.

"Humph! Well she don't have to instruct *me* how much butter to let cook use in her sauce, and so I nearly told her to her face."

Susan did not ask her aunt to dissuade Julia from these intrusions into the domestic affairs of Mansfield; she knew that Lady Bertram would only reply, "Oh, that is very tiresome of dear Julia to be sure, but Whittemore must not mind it; now, where did I lay down my sea-green worsted?"

At the time when she first came to Mansfield, Susan Price had been a well-grown, hot-tempered, good-hearted girl of fourteen. The society of Northamptonshire could not find her handsome; well-grown for her age she was allowed to be, and she had a fair degree of countenance; but her features were too pronounced and her neck too long and her hair too lank. Her complexion was by far too brown, and she would never match her cousins in looks.—The passage of a few years amended some of these faults. She was now admitted by many to be a remarkably fine girl; but still some of these would sigh, and add, "Ah, she will never be the equal of her cousin Maria; Miss Maria Bertram was the beauty of Northamptonshire."

The said Maria Bertram had made an unfortunate marriage to a heavy, dull young man of considerable fortune, whom she had never respected, and rapidly learned to despise; after less than a year of marriage she had quitted his establishment for another man, and, when her husband divorced her and her lover left her, she had gone to live in retirement and reproach, at a considerable distance from Northamptonshire, companioned by an aunt whose strong attachment to her as a child had only been strengthened further by her disgrace and banishment from good society.

Miss Maria's name was never spoken at Mansfield. Her father had utterly forbidden it. A man of high principle and strong moral judgment, he had suffered anguish unspeakable at the time of his daughter's degradation, feeling that some lack of basic guidance, some gross error in early teaching, must place the blame on *his* shoulders as a parent; sensible of this blame he naturally detested the cause of it, and could not bear the least allusion to any topic bordering on reference to his abandoned daughter.

Lady Bertram was not so nice. Never, even when they were small, having been deeply attached to her children, she felt much less interest in them as they grew older, and had long ago divested herself of any anxieties or gratification regarding them, unless in a matter directly concerning herself. And as to her grandchildren, her chief wish was that they should not crumple her gown, tangle her embroidery silk, or frighten Pug.

That Lady Bertram never alluded to the erring Maria was due primarily to a complete lack of interest in her disgraced daughter's fortunes; in fact she was hardly remembered from one year's end to another.

Lady Bertram could, however, when it occurred to her, display some concern for those immediately connected to her daily life; this care for others was now manifested by her turning to Susan, as she rose to go and dress for dinner, in order to inquire,

"Should I send Chapman to help Fanny pack for the West Indies, Susan? She could go over when she has dressed me. Do you think it would be of assistance to Fanny if I sent Chapman?"

"No, ma'am, that is kind of you, but I believe she is already as well forward as need be, with the help of her Rachel and a girl from the village."

Her mind thus lightened from care, Lady Bertram proceeded upstairs, and Susan was on the point of following when Tom and Edmund came back from the estate-room, still deep in the discussion of agricultural drills and new breeds of cattle.

"We are agreed as to the pastures beyond Easton, then. I shall expect to hear from you that the sheep do well on them.—Why,

Cousin Susan, has my mother gone up already? I had no notion it was so late. Fanny will be wondering where I have got to. I will take my leave, then, Tom—"

"If I can take up a moment of your time, Cousin Edmund—" began Susan, with a diffidence which hardly bore out the recent views of her expressed by Mrs. Yates, "I was hoping to catch you before you went—"

Edmund, with all the kindness of an excellent nature, immediately stopped and asked how he could help his cousin?

From her first arrival at Mansfield, Edmund had felt an esteem for his wife's sister, observing with what energy and goodwill she had taken over the not inconsiderable task of keeping his mother occupied and entertained; this admiration had, in the course of time, ripened into a strong and warm affection. Of a quiet and sober disposition himself, and married to the equally tranquil and gentle Fanny, he could yet admire the liveliness of Susan's nature, and the way in which she found diversion and kept herself amused at Mansfield, despite the grave atmosphere and general want of animation in the household.

"I was wishing before you went away to ascertain your views regarding this business of my cousin Maria," said Susan with her usual directness.

Both brothers stared at her in surprise.

"How in the world did you get wind of *that?*" burst out Tom, with no small vexation in his tone. "And what business, may I ask, Cousin Susan, do you consider it to be of yours?"

Looking at his red, affronted countenance, Susan realised that she had erred in not addressing herself to the elder brother, who now felt that his authority as new head of the family had been set aside. Quickly, she did her best to rectify this mistake.

"That is—I was wanting to ask the opinion of you both—but in recent months Edmund has been so much more in my aunt's company than you have, Tom, that I addressed myself to him as being likelier to judge of her present sentiments in the matter. I am anxious to know how you both feel: should my aunt be told of this new development? Or do you think that would be to distress her unnecessarily?"

The new Sir Thomas hardly seemed much conciliated by having his opinion thus canvassed. Susan had a suspicion that he would have preferred to be given the dignity of his new title and not addressed with such cousinly informality as *Tom.* He repeated, in a colder tone,

"May I ask, cousin, by what means the tale came to your ears? I was not aware that it had been generally bruited abroad. And I feel most strongly that the less said about this matter, the better."

"Who could argue with that?" replied Susan calmly. "I can assure you, cousin, that I have not the least intention of *bruiting the news abroad.* It is indeed of no personal interest to me, never having met my cousin Maria. I merely wished to consult you and Edmund as to whether you think it best that your mother be kept in the dark about it—with the consequent risk that some gossip-loving neighbour who has read a paragraph in the newspaper may come out with a remark or inquiry, under the assumption that Lady Bertram has been fully informed of the matter."

"The decision is a difficult one," replied Edmund, after some deliberation, and seeing that Tom remained silent. "What do you think, Tom? Is it your opinion that our mother would be greatly distressed at having the past reopened? May not these tidings of Maria recall to Mamma the fact that at the time of my sister's disgrace our father was still living, and so aggravate the wound and increase her grief at our present loss?"

Tom looked serious.

"Our mother has received the news of his death with consider-able fortitude," said he after a pause.

Susan reflected that for *fortitude* might almost be substituted the word *insensibility*. Already accustomed, after a four-months' absence from home, to the lack of her husband's daily appearance at the head of the table, or at the tea-board in the evening, Lady Bertram seemed hardly yet to have assimilated the *nevermore* comprised in the tidings of his death; she sighed at times and said, "How we need Sir Thomas," but without any stronger conviction in her voice than if he had merely departed on a somewhat longer voyage than had been anticipated.

"Perhaps we should ask Julia's opinion," Tom went on.

"I do not believe." said Edmund impatiently, "that my sister Julia has a deeper insight, a minuter or juster knowledge of my mother's state of mind than anybody here present. What do you think yourself, Susan?"

"I should be in favour of telling her the whole," replied Susan without hesitation. "In that way, the moment of revelation can be chosen with due care and discretion, at a time when my aunt is in calm spirits and not beset by anxieties, when she will have ample leisure for reflection, and can, if she needs, comfort herself by directing her thoughts to other subjects. If that is done, it need not be too much of a shock to her."

"Upon reflection, I believe you are right," said Edmund. "My mother's mind works slowly; it will be best that she should have a period of time in privacy, or with one of the close family circle to advise and talk over the matter; yes, I believe that she should be informed, at a judiciously chosen moment. What do you say, Tom?"

"What *I* should like to know," said Tom, without answering his brother's question, "what I should like to know is how Susan ever came by this information?"

"Why, how do you think? Fanny told me just now when I was helping her pack up her things," cried out Susan hastily, as if she could hardly believe that he had not the wit to work out such a simple solution for himself. "How in the world else should you imagine I might have heard it, Cousin Tom? By carrier pigeon?"

On her first arrival at Mansfield, Susan had been much given to such little quicknesses and broadnesses of utterance, freedoms of speech to which she had been accustomed at home in Portsmouth, among her brothers. Awe at the splendour of her new surroundings, and a quick ear, had soon assisted her to a greater elegance and propriety of diction, modelled on the soft, clear gentle speech of her elder sister Fanny. But there were still occasions when her tongue betrayed her and moved more swiftly than her wiser sense; when impatience brought in a reversion to that earlier, sharper way of speaking; these moments were becoming less and less frequent, for Susan herself could not have been more conscious of their impropriety; at each lapse she would blush inwardly and castigate herself for her loss of control, resolving to be infinitely more careful in future, to let no unbidden word leave her lips. In nine cases out of ten, the cause of these little roughnesses of manner would be an argument with her cousin Tom. Somehow, with neither side particularly intending it, the two cousins contrived to irritate one another. Tom had always, if only half consciously, felt Susan as an intruder at Mansfield, and never troubled himself to try and overcome this sentiment, irrational though it might be; while Susan had strong, though unexpressed objections in regard to Tom's rather lordly air of patronage towards herself. The authority of her aunt and uncle she was naturally glad to

acknowledge, since towards them, for their hospitality and benevolence, she felt a deep gratitude and sense of obligation; any
commands of theirs she would make haste to obey; but she felt no
obligation laid on her to obey such commands as might emanate
from Tom, and had no hesitation in making this plain.

Quick-witted and intelligent, used to dealing with her lively
brothers, Susan was easily a match in argument for her cousin Tom,
who had never been more than ordinarily clever and had generally
been excelled at school by his younger brother Edmund. When
Susan first arrived at Mansfield, Tom, then aged twenty-six, had
been slowly recovering from a dangerous fever; greatly reduced and
weakened he had, for a short time, been pleased enough to have the
companionship of the plain, eager, lively fourteen-year-old girl, who
was friendly, ready and willing to play chess with him, read to him,
or entertain him in any way he wished. But as his strength returned,
so did the urge to dominate; Tom had always been used to command
his younger sisters, and his delicate little shrinking cousin Fanny; he
was good-natured enough and often gave them presents, but he was
accustomed to lord it; he expected a more subservient and
complaisant attitude from Susan than she was prepared to yield;
indeed she was not prepared to yield to her cousin Tom at all,
finding him in all respects except for looks, greatly inferior to his
brother.—Recovered from the fever, Tom was certainly a fine young
man of pleasing air and appearance, open-faced, fresh-coloured,
well-set-up, cheerful and obliging so long as he had his own way,
and prepared to enter heartily into other people's interests so long as
they coincided with his own.—But in all deeper and more serious
aspects, Susan considered Edmund infinitely superior; Edmund was
a reading, judging, thinking person, an original intellect, a nature of

just and strong principle. Whereas the nature of Tom was shallower, or at any rate had not yet been stirred to any very profound reflection, even during the time of his serious indisposition.

In many small ways, without particularly intending to, Susan had contrived to indicate her poor opinion of her elder cousin; and his retaliation was to make plain the fact that he considered her an intruder, from an undesirable, indigent background, of inferior status to the Mansfield family. This attitude he had managed to transmit to his sister Julia, who, though selfishly glad that no part of the care for Lady Bertram devolved on her, yet felt it a grievance that somebody with no right of birth should be enjoying the benefits of Mansfield.

When she was younger Tom had teased Susan about her plain looks, addressing her as *Miss Bones* and *Mouse-locks,* though not in the hearing of his father. During the past six or seven months Tom had been away from home so much that the improvement in his cousin's figure and countenance had come to him as a considerable surprise on his return. In that regard he could no longer find fault, but this could almost be felt as an additional annoyance, along with what he chose to consider her unjustified self-assurance.

"*Fanny* gave you the news about my sister Maria?" he now demanded.

"If you recall, brother," said Edmund hastily, "Fanny was with us when Frank Wadham gave us the information. Fanny has been acquainted with the whole matter from the start."

"True. She was there. I had forgot."

The news in question being that their disgraced sister Maria had recently seen fit to quit her secluded country abode and remove herself to London. The cause of this, and means whereby it had been achieved, were the death of the widowed Aunt Norris, sister to Lady

Bertram, with whom Maria had for some years resided. About six months previously Mrs. Norris had succumbed to an affection of the lungs and, dying, had bequeathed her entire fortune to her beloved niece. Since Mrs. Norris' disposition had been a particularly thrifty and frugal one, the fortune in question proved to be of quite ample size, some eight and a half thousand pounds. Thus endowed and freed at the same time from her watch-dog and chaperon, Maria had no hesitation in disposing of her small country house and finding herself lodgings in Upper Seymour Street, not far from a set of unsteady and pleasure-loving friends from former times, the Aylmers. In London, it was greatly to be apprehended, since the former Mrs. Rushworth could not be received in polite circles, and did not choose to remain in solitude, she could only of necessity mix in a highly questionable part of society, and must be a source of mortification and anxiety to her sundered family, who might justifiably wonder what scrape she would fall into next. The best to be hoped was that she might scramble into matrimony with some elderly man, not too nice in his judgments, and vain enough to set store by the connection with one who was still an acknowledged beauty, though of blemished character.

This news had been brought to Mansfield by the Reverend Francis Wadham, Edmund's friend who was to take over his parochial duties during his absence in the West Indies.

Mr. Wadham was not personally acquainted with the former Miss Bertram, but his widowed sister Mrs. Osborne had been a neighbour of the two ladies in their Cumberland seclusion, and a kind and attentive neighbour, furthermore, who had done all in her power to render assistance and give comfort during the last wretched weeks of Mrs. Norris's life. After that lady's death, also, Mrs. Osborne had endeavoured to continue in her friendly offices to the bereaved niece, and had advised her most fervently and earnestly against the move to town; but all such counsel fell on deaf ears; Maria had only been waiting for this opportunity. Another three or four weeks saw her and all her belongings transferred from Keswick to Upper Seymour Street.—Of this Mr. Wadham had been able to inform Edmund and Fanny Bertram when he came to Mansfield Parsonage.

Who would be the proper person to inform Lady Bertram of her daughter's action, was the next question to be discussed among the three cousins.

"Wadham's sister herself, the Mrs. Osborne in question, is coming soon to keep house for him while he is at the Parsonage." said Edmund. "She is a most excellent person: intelligent, gentle, unaffected, and sensible. She is the widow of an admiral, Admiral Giles Osborne. I think Mrs. Osborne will make a valuable older friend for Susan while Fanny is overseas; and perhaps, as she has been poor Maria's neighbour, and has seen her lately, *she* may be thought the best person to impart this agitating news to my mother."

Tom, however, was wholly opposed to this suggestion. What! a complete stranger! a woman whom none of the family had met, or even heard of before that day, to be communicating such a particularly delicate and distressing piece of news! "Good heaven, Edmund, what can you be thinking of? This Mrs. Osborne is, I daresay, well enough in her way, a decent enough sort of woman—but for an outsider to be meddling in a matter such as this, is not to be thought of!"

"Then you had best do it yourself, Tom," said Edmund calmly.

Tom hemmed and hawed at this.—He was not on such confidential terms with his mother as to justify his being the one to make such a revelation—thought in any case the information would be best imparted by a female—a female would know best how to break the disagreeable news without imparting too much of a shock. Without any doubt—thinking the matter over—Fanny would be the most suitable person for such a task. Yes, Fanny had better do it. She was the right, the only person.

The only drawback to this scheme being that Fanny and Edmund were due to quit Mansfield at eight o'clock the following morning, long before Lady Bertram had even left her chamber.

"Well then," said Tom, when finally brought to accept this inconvenient fact, "there is nothing for it. Julia must tell my mother. Yes, that will be best. Julia, after all, is Maria's own sister, she must be thought to have the greatest interest in the matter. I will send a note over to Shawcross, and ask Julia to come tomorrow. I daresay my mother will be glad of a visit from her tomorrow, in any case; she must be missing Fanny."

Having thus satisfied himself, Tom went away to write the note.

The other two were less convinced that Julia would be the right person, but, knowing Tom would not be happy unless he felt the decision was left to him, were content to leave it so, since both of them had many affairs of their own to attend to, Edmund the last details of his packing, and Susan the arrangements for the reception of her little niece.—They bade each other an affectionate farewell and swiftly separated.

Tom's note to his sister, imparting the news of the disgraced Maria's removal to London, and asking Julia to divulge it to Lady Bertram, met with an extremely curt refusal. Mrs. Yates had no interest in her sister's present position or whereabouts, and saw no reason why she should be saddled with the task of disclosing the matter to her mother. Let Susan do it if the thing must be done; for which, on her part, she saw not the slightest necessity.

In the end, therefore, it was Susan, who, handing back her aunt's netting with all the tangles straightened out, ready to be retangled, said calmly,

"Aunt Bertram, I have a piece of news to give you."

"What is that, my dear? Nothing dreadful has happened to Edmund and Fanny and dear little William?"

"No, ma'am, nothing of that kind. It relates to my cousin Maria. Since Aunt Norris died, she has sold the house in Cumberland which my uncle bought her, and has removed to London."

"Indeed?" remarked Maria's mother languidly. "To what part of London?"

"To Upper Seymour Street, Edmund told me."

"Ah. I am not familiar with that street. When the children were small, and Sir Thomas was in Parliament, we were used, in the season, to take a house in Grosvenor Square; but I found the journeys to London too tiring; I began to find it too tiring; and so we gave up the habit. I take no pleasure in London. There are too many strangers. We go on far better in the country, seeing only those we know. Ring the bell, Susan, I want my dinner. Tom must be dressed by this time."

Susan smiled to herself, as she obeyed her aunt, recalling all the foresight and caution that had been wasted on this slight exchange.

Chapter 2

SUSAN THOUGHT IT PROPER, SO SOON AS MRS. YATES PAID HER next visit to Mansfield, and she could be spared from an hour's attendance on Lady Bertram, to walk across the park and call at the Parsonage.

By this time Mrs. Osborne had arrived, and was installed as lady of the house. Her brother, the Reverend Francis, Susan had already met on the previous Sunday in Edmund's company: he was a sensible, interesting, gentlemanlike man in his early thirties, rather thin and pale from the illness that had obliged him to return from his missionary duties; he greeted Susan, when she arrived at the Parsonage, with every kind attention, and asked leave to introduce his sister. Mrs. Osborne, some five years older than her brother, was very similar to him in feature: she had the same long, rather serious cast of countenance; that of Mrs. Osborne suggested that she had spent many years with her husband at sea; she was deeply tanned, and her hair, somewhat untidily arranged, had turned prematurely white. She met Susan with unaffected interest, exclaiming, "Ah, my dear, how glad I am to know you! I have heard so much about you from your cousin Edmund. How young and pretty you are to have such a household on your shoulders! But I can see that, though different in appearance from your sister, you share her practical judgment and good sense."

Susan laughed, blushed, and disclaimed. "It is all made easy for me there, ma'am; I only pass on my aunt Bertram's wishes to the housekeeper."

In no time she found herself conversing with Mr. Wadham and his sister as with old friends; there was a bewitching charm and informality about their manners which contrasted strongly with the sobriety to be found within the confines of Mansfield, and which greatly raised her spirits, depressed at the six-months' parting from Fanny and Edmund, besides the prospect of being, during the ensuing period, principally in the company of Tom Bertram and Mrs. Yates. But now—with this delightful company to be found just across the park—she need have no apprehension of loneliness or lack of counsel.

"You must feel us as shocking intruders in your sister's house," Mrs. Osborne said. "I have probably put all her favourite plants in the wrong places. I am a sad, heedless housekeeper. Pray, Miss Price, do not stand upon ceremony; walk about the house as if Mrs. Bertram were here, and, if you see anything out of place, do not hesitate to move it back."

"No, ma'am, I have no wish to do so, I assure you; everything looks charmingly; it is a pleasure to see the house in such good hands."

Mr. Wadham presently excused himself to be off about his duties in the parish, and Susan soon after rose to take her leave, explaining that she could not be absent from her aunt for too long.

"May I walk back with you across the park?" inquired Mrs. Osborne. "That would be such a pleasure. I am used to take long walks and rides every day, in Cumberland, you know, where it is so wild that the sight of an unescorted lady causes no remark because there is nobody to see her; one may walk for twenty miles and never encounter a soul. Here it is not so, I am aware, and I have promised Frank to curtail my walks. He, poor fellow, is still weak, and soon knocked up; I cannot expect him to escort me just yet except in the barouche."

Susan was happy to have her company and the two ladies crossed the park at a quick pace. The month was April, and Mrs. Osborne exclaimed at how much further advanced the season was here than in the countryside she had left behind.

"There, you know, Miss Price, winter lasts until mid May; but here, how fresh, how green everything appears. What a charming prospect across these lawns and plantations. You are lucky to live amid such scenes."

"I am fully aware of that.' said Susan. "Until I was fourteen, you know, I lived in a city, in Portsmouth. I was accustomed only to crowds, incessant noise, dirt, and confusion. Even after four years my awareness, my gratitude for the alteration in my circumstances has not abated in the slightest degree; I feel it every day. I love Mansfield dearly."

Mrs. Osborne smiled in friendly approval of this sentiment. "I believe," she said, "that Mansfield has a particular charm, a particular power to instil affection into the hearts of those who reside here. Some months since, as I believe you may know, I was able to be of service to a sick lady—your aunt, Mrs. Norris. Towards the end, her illness had affected her mind, she was greatly confused and wandering a great deal of the time; all the while I sat with her, in her delirium, she would be talking of Mansfield, its walks, its shrubberies, its lawns and gates; she missed it sadly, I am sure, poor lady, and yearned to be back here."

Susan was much struck by this. "How very sad! My poor aunt Norris. I did not know that she was so attached to the place. I was not well acquainted with my aunt; she quitted Mansfield very shortly after I arrived here."

Susan could have added that the departure of her aunt Norris was a source of unalloyed relief, since her aunt had taken a strong dislike to the newly arrived niece and lost no opportunity of bestowing snubs, sharp remarks, and slighting references to *poor and pushing relations*. But there was no purpose in speaking ill of the dead. She said instead, "Aunt Norris was very devoted to my cousin Maria, I collect. She must at least have been happy to die in her company."

Mrs. Osborne looked doubtful. "Your cousin Maria—have you ever met her?"

"No, I have not."

"She is of a strong, impatient disposition, not the most suitable, perhaps, for care of a sick person. Latterly she was not much in company with your aunt; she was not equal to the requirements of invalid care, and the vagaries and ramblings of Mrs. Norris worried and wore her out; some people are like that; they find a sick-room too taxing. Your aunt, I think, had been a very strong, active character, when in good health?"

"So I understand."

"Her niece, perhaps, had relied upon her and depended on her; then she found it too difficult when the positions were reversed and she herself was called upon to be the supporter."

"I fancy," said Susan, thinking of Maria's sister Julia, and of how little use *she* was likely to be in a sick-room, "I fancy that my aunt Norris was very lucky to have you, ma'am, as a neighbour and friend during her last illness."

"Oh, my dear. I have been used to so many vicissitudes! On board ship, you know—and most of my life has been spent on board ship—there is always somebody in need of care. I have nursed a great quantity of midshipmen, lieutenants, even captains, in my time; I looked to nurse my poor husband in his last illness, and it was a sad shock when he was swept overboard by a wave in the North Seas.—But your aunt Norris I believe would have been very glad to return to Mansfield. Very frequently in her latter days she would be mistaking me for her sister Lady Bertram. 'It is time the girls should have a ball at Mansfield, sister,' she has said to me, twenty times over, and I always replied, 'They shall have one, Mrs. Norris, as soon as you are back on your feet and cook has made sufficient white soup.'"

"Ah, poor soul," cried Susan, touched by this story. "It will be very kind in you, Mrs. Osborne, to talk with my aunt Bertram some time about her sister, and tell her some of these memories. But, I think, not quite yet; my uncle's death, and the departure of my sister and her husband, have been heavy burdens on my aunt—her mental constitution is not robust—"

"I would not dream of troubling her with sad recollections at present." quickly replied Mrs. Osborne. "Only let me know when my presence would be acceptable, and I shall be happy to wait upon her.—Ah, is that the White House over there?"—pointing across the park to where the thatched roofs of Mansfield village could be seen, and one house somewhat larger than the rest. "So many, many times your poor aunt would be talking about the White House. 'It is not a large habitation, but just of a size to support the rank of gentlewoman, with one modest-sized reception room and a spare room for a friend—' So often she has described house and garden that I could almost have sketched the place from memory! Who lives there now?"

"Why, no one at present," said Susan. "An old tutor of my cousins was living there for some time, but he removed to be with his brother at Padstowe. My cousin Tom wishes to let the house, and has put it in the hands of his agent Mr. Claypole.—Dear me, here is my cousin Mrs. Yates. I am rather surprised that she should have left my aunt alone."

Julia was to be seen on the carriage sweep in front of the house, calling her little boys, who were throwing stones at the lilies in the lily-pond.

"*There* you are, Susan! At last! I am sure I have been waiting for you this hour, until Tommy and Johnny were quite out of patience—for my mother, you know, soon becomes fatigued in their company, and they are not used, poor little fellows, to sit quiet as mice indoors without moving a finger—and Lady Bertram would have it that Johnny stuck a needle into Pug, which is not possible since he was quite at the other end of the room, good as gold, looking at a book of engravings—and then Tom came in, and was quite unreasonable; so I have left *him* with my mother, and went to inform Whittemore of the scandalous tales I have heard from Galloway about the way the Mansfield under-servants behave in church—"

Julia had cast one careless, slighting look at Susan's companion, and then, continuing to deliver this tirade, ignored her completely, as if she were of no account. Susan, mortified at such behavior, endeavoured to cut short the flow.

"Cousin Julia, let me make known to you Mrs. Osborne, Mr. Wadham's sister, from the Parsonage."

At this reminder, clearly given, Mrs. Yates did recall her manners, and gave utterance to a few perfunctory and meaningless civilities, very artificially delivered. To these Mrs. Osborne replied with remarks of considerably more genuine value, and concluded by hoping to have the pleasure of waiting upon Lady Bertram within a few days. Then, taking a very friendly leave of Susan, Mrs. Osborne turned back the way they had come, walking at a quick pace.

"Good heaven! What a very odd-looking woman!" said Julia, glancing after her. "Really, when you first appeared with her, I thought she must be some old retired governess or laundry-woman. What a figure she makes of herself! No one would believe that Admiral Osborne left her over eighty thousand pounds when he died—yet such I have heard to be the case. But those persons connected with the Navy are all the same—no style, no manners, no elegance. I suppose she will now be expecting to effect an *entrée* into Mansfield—'Wait on Lady Bertram,' indeed. Such impertinence! What pleasure, what conversation, what interest can *she* have to offer my mother? *That* is hardly an acquaintance to be encouraged. I suppose we shall be obliged to receive the brother, since he is to conduct the service on Sundays, but I confess I do not see the necessity of including such a person as that in our circle. It is rather hard that she should force herself upon us."

Susan felt herself so wholly in opposition to all the sentiments here uttered that she was greatly relieved when at this moment little Johnny, over-reaching himself, fell into the lily-pond to be rescued amid screams and splashes.

Julia shortly thereafter taking her departure with her children, the subject of Mrs. Osborne did not arise again upon that day.

Chapter 3

ABOUT TEN DAYS AFTER THE FOREGOING EVENTS, SUSAN WAS IN the flower-garden with little Mary, picking a bunch of hyacinths to take to her aunt Bertram, when, glancing over the paling, she saw two figures approaching through the park, who, on a closer view, proved to be Mr. Wadham with his sister. As Lady Bertram had been left in a comfortable doze, from which it seemed unlikely that she would awake within the hour, Susan had no hesitation in walking out to meet the pair.

"Good day, Miss Susan! How do you go on!" Mr. Wadham hailed her cheerfully as soon as they were within speaking distance. "The weather is so fine that my sister has tempted me this way. We are acting as postmen—bringing you a letter that has come for your sister."

"For my sister? Why, who can be writing to her at the Parsonage? All in our family—my mother and those at Portsmouth, my brother William in the Navy—everybody has been informed that she has gone abroad. I wonder who her correspondent can be?"

Then Susan recalled an old teacher, Miss Quantrell, who had taught both Fanny and herself, and who occasionally sent a letter to one or the other of them. She slipped the letter into her pocket for later investigation. Fanny had left instructions that if any correspondence of an unexpected nature should arrive, Susan was to open letters and use her own judgment as to whether they should be forwarded on to Antigua or retained in England for her return.

"Are you finding life pleasant at the Parsonage?" she then inquired. "Do the servants give satisfaction?"

"Oh, my dear! They spoil us to death. Your sister Fanny's Rachel is a treasure! And the garden is so pretty, now warm days are here. Frank sits in the conservatory and I sit in the garden. But Frank is mending fast, as you see: this is the first day that he has felt strong enough to walk right across the park."

"Mr. Wadham does look better," said Susan. "He has more colour. But you must not over-exert yourself. Had you not better come into the house, after such a long walk, and take some refreshment? I know my cousin Edmund would wish it—"

Mr. Wadham and his sister looked at one another a little doubtingly. It was plain that Julia Yates's lack of civility had not been thrown away on Mrs. Osborne, and that the pair had no intention of intruding where they were not perfectly welcome. At that moment, however, Tom Bertram rode round the curve of the driveway, returning from a survey of his coverts, and gave the parson and his sister a very friendly welcome. Sociable, company-loving Tom was feeling the lack of male society, which London, Bath, and Harrowgate had afforded him in such plenty; he had decided that the new incumbent was a decent, gentlemanlike fellow enough, and was disposed to welcome his presence.

"Why do not you step upstairs to the drawing-room and make yourself known to my mother, ma'am?" he urged Mrs. Osborne.

"Susan will take you, will you not, cousin? For sure, my mother will be overjoyed to have a caller; she has been fairly moped since my brother and his wife went overseas.'

So while Tom showed his visitor the billiard-room and sent for a bottle of Madeira, Susan led Mrs. Osborne upstairs to where Lady Bertram reclined upon her sopha.

That lady had just awakened from her doze, and for a moment or two appeared slightly confused.

"What is it? What is the matter?" she asked, in a voice thickened by sleep; but, Mrs. Osborne sitting down by her in a most friendly way, quite lacking in ceremony, and engaging her in conversation about the work that she was at present embarked on (a net purse), she presently brightened up to a remarkable degree. Susan, entertaining little Mary with coloured blocks at the far end of the room, heard with something approaching awe how Mrs. Osborne drew her hostess on to discuss crewel-work, tatting, the best method of making fringe, the best use for fringe when made, the salient differences between *petit* and *gros* point, and a vast quantity of related topics.

"I have not been used to occupy myself greatly with such hand-work, ma'am, until quite recently, after my poor husband the admiral was washed overboard, but, I assure you, the sailors on his ships used to engage in a wonderful variety of such occupations—knitting and knotting and netting—it would quite do your heart good to see them at it, their tarry fingers so neat and dexterous with the twine or hemp or whatever it might be. And they were for ever presenting me with knitting-needles and netting-pins, the dear fellows! Many a clever contrivance have I learned from some honest able-seaman, and I shall be more than happy, ma'am, to pass on some of my acquisitions to you."

From descriptions of the sailors' ingenious occupations, it was an easy transition to tales of naval occasions, of which Mrs. Osborne appeared to have an unlimited supply, for during her eighteen years of happy marriage she had crossed the Atlantic four times, encircled the Mediterranean, and sailed round the Cape of Good Hope to the East Indies. Susan herself listened with unaffected interest to these tales, which were told with great liveliness and simplicity; and Lady Bertram, quite captivated, reclined on her sopha, the forgotten piece of netting slid from her hand, her eyes, fully opened for once, fixed on distance as she attempted to envisage the scenes described to her.—She had probably never been half so well entertained in her life before.

By and bye Susan recalled the letter which Mrs. Osborne had been on the way to bring her. Little Mary, having built a palace with her blocks, had crept up to the sopha, and, also falling under the strange lady's spell, was sitting curled up with her thumb in her mouth, leaning against her grandmother's skirts.

Susan therefore quietly drew the letter from her pocket and surveyed the direction.—The hand was not familiar to her. A paper-knife at hand upon the table—"Fanny would certainly wish that it be opened, in case it contained some request, or instruction, that needed carrying out immediately" was Susan's final conclusion.

She opened the letter and began to read. The handwriting was shaky—at first she found it difficult to make out. But by degrees she became accustomed.

My very dear, my dearest Fanny:
You will start, I daresay, to see this hand. Perhaps you will have forgotten it quite. So many years have passed since I last penned a note to you, and you will

have so many other pressing concerns, so many other correspondents, in your busy, happy, active life at Mansfield. Sweet, charming Mansfield! My pen forms that word with greater ease than any other, even now, even after so long a removal. I never spent so happy a summer as the one that was passed within its quiet confines, and to the uttermost end of my life I shall regret the action—the series of hasty imprudent actions—that severed me from the life of Mansfield, and all that Mansfield entails. Mansfield, to me, will always spell perfection.

Well, you will be demanding, Fanny, what all this is about; I see your wondering look. Have you forgot your old friend Mary Crawford, with whom you were used to spend so many agreeable, if not instructive, hours, idling about the shrubberies of Mansfield Parsonage? Have you forgot the mare, and how I shamelessly and selfishly robbed you of her use for hours together in those happy summer days? Have you forgot the ball at Mansfield, and how we danced our shoes to tatters? You were the belle of the evening, Fanny, and I remember you yet, in your white dress with the shining dots, and the gold necklace you wore, and the poor heart that beat for you in vain! But I will not tease you, good, gentle Fanny; events fall out as they must, no doubt, and the prize you won in the great lottery was better by far than my poor wayward brother—who remains to this day a bachelor because he can find no lady in the fashionable world equal to replace hard-hearted Fanny.

Yes, you may stare, but so it is. Henry has never married. The most cunning snares, the wiliest lures have failed to capture him. With such a memory to fortify his heart, he is far too nice for the gilded paroquets of London society; indeed, he spends the greater part of the year improving his acres at Everingham.

As to myself—the sad tale is soon told. I married to disoblige myself.—At the time, it seemed an excellent match. My sister, Mrs. Grant, was by no means opposed to the connection. But then she, poor dear, was greatly pulled down, at that period, by the complaint that soon afterwards carried her off, and, I dare say, was anxious to see me well settled. The man I married, Sir Charles Ormiston, *seemed* well-disposed and unexceptionable; not handsome, somewhat older than myself, but gentlemanlike, and of a fortune sufficient to command respect. But how was I taken in! I soon discovered that the appearance was but a hollow façade; he was an indolent, selfish *bon-vivant,* and not only that but a truly vicious man, of libertine propensities. I will not distress your ears, Fanny, by a recital of my sufferings at his hands. Suffice it to say that, though severe, they are over now: Sir Charles is not dead, but has to be confined, for his mind has broken down under the strain of a lifetime's excesses and dissipations. At me, he can no longer rave; he raves at his family's expense, immured in a distant wing of Ormiston House. Do not shudder, Fanny, he brought it on himself. He deserved no better.

What of myself, you ask, and the answer is no cheerful one. I have been unwell—very unwell; for a period my life was given up. Only the fond solicitude of my brother Henry, who sat for days and nights on end by my couch, holding my hand, begging, beseeching me not to leave him—only his dear affection recalled me to this earthly vale; and whether the boon of restored life he thus conferred on me was worth his pains, who can judge? Not I, indeed. At present I am still far, very far, from complete health. My physician has prescribed country air. Ormiston House is horrible to me, Henry's estate at Everingham, in the doctor's judgment, too bracing. Where, then, to settle for a few recuperative months?

Can you wonder, Fanny, that my heart has been turning fondly, very fondly, to memories of the glades, the paths, the lawns of Mansfield, to the sweet air that breathes above those leafy groves and verdant plantations?

In truth, dear Fanny, it is not only the *place* that summons me. Apart from my brother, and my deceased sister, the two dearest, truest friends, the purest and most wholesome influences that in my short and misspent life I ever encountered, have been yourself and your husband. Can you and Mr. Edmund Bertram—I write his name with a faltering hand—can you bring yourselves to overlook the errors of the past, can you forgive your faulty but sincerely affectionate friend? I do truly believe that only your conversation—your wise, grave earnest elevating companionship—intercourse untouched by guile or artifice—can now restore the tone of my mind. Can I ask this of you? May I be received at Mansfield?

A single line, Fanny—a single word—will bring this scheme to a halt. You have only to despatch the word *No,* to your troubled friend, and she will abandon the plan entirely. It may be too much to ask. But if not—if you and Edmund—there, I have writ his name again—if you, in your plenty, can spare a crumb or two from your well-spread table, I believe you will be doing a work equal in benevolence to any of your daily duties among the fortunate parishioners at Mansfield.

Henry, devoted brother as he is, has already ascertained that there is a house to be let in the village: the White House. (In the old days I believe this was where Lady Bertram's sister was used to reside; I do not recall her name.) If I hear nothing from you, Fanny—if a *No* does not come through the post to dash my poor hopes—Henry purposes to escort me to Mansfield in mid May, and leave me there ensconced. He, too, I will not deny, is eager to revisit the scenes of so much happiness—alas, of so much lost happiness.

Your affectionate friend from old times,

Mary Crawford

P.S. I sign myself so because I detest the name of Ormiston and will never, if I can avoid doing so, hear it again. I prefer the older appellation, and love best those who address me as M. C.

It may well be supposed in what a state of perturbation and astonishment Susan read through the foregoing lines. The letter was not one to be perused once only—as soon as she had finished, Susan began it again. *Ah, poor thing!* was her first thought; here, apparently, was this Miss Crawford, longing, pining to see Fanny and Edmund, persuaded that they, and they alone, with their elevating companionship, could restore her to health; unaware that, at the time of her solicitation, they were five thousand miles away, and would not be returning to Mansfield for many months.

I must write *immediately* and inform Miss Crawford—or rather Lady Ormiston—was Susan's first hasty resolution. I must break it to her, as quickly as possible, that her hopes are vain, that they are based on a false premise. How wretchedly afflicted she will be at the news. For there seems such an urgency—almost an air of life-and-death about the letter. I only hope that the disappointment may not bring on a serious relapse in the unfortunate lady's health.

She looked back, then, to the date at the opening, and discovered that the letter must have been several days upon the way, and had lain, perhaps, a day or two at the Parsonage before being carried to her. In fact it was now almost—perhaps quite—too late to countermand the arrangements which were already in process of making.— Now that Susan recollected the matter indeed, she thought she remembered hearing Tom remark with satisfaction that the White House was let at last; Claypole, his agent, had found a pair of eligible tenants. Servants had arrived; the house was about to be opened up.

Susan had reached this point in her reflections when they were broken in upon by Mrs. Osborne, who now stood up to take her leave.

"I fancy, Miss Price, that I have tired your aunt quite long enough with my chatter; but we have had such a charming gossip that I quite forgot the time. I had better run away and rescue Mr. Bertram from my brother, who quite doats on billiards and will be here for ever if he is not forcibly removed. Lady Bertram, I will wish you good day, and shall hope to have the pleasure of demonstrating that feather-stitch to you when I can persuade my brother to bring me this way again."

Susan escorted the caller downstairs, and on the way expressed her warm gratitude for the very real amusement and distraction that the visit had afforded to her aunt.

"Her life is so remarkably quiet that she falls into a lassitude; but I believe a little mental exertion, such as listening to your very enter-taining conversation, ma'am, does her all the good in the world."

Mrs. Osborne laughed very heartily at the notion of her conver-sation being thought to provide mental exertion.

"If my chat is of benefit to her, Miss Price, she may have it again whenever she chuses. I will engage to prose on for ever about the Streights and the Forties, the Bermudas and the Bahamas; it is always a pleasure to me to recall those times."

Her sensible, benevolent face was, indeed, lit with happiness at the mere recollection; and Susan was forcibly struck by the contrast between such a well-spent life, whose minutest event could be recalled with interest and pleasure or profit; and that of Fanny's correspondent, Mary Crawford, who seemed basing her every hope and prospect of recovery from illness on the memory of a few summer months passed at Mansfield, during a life otherwise wasted in trifling, unprofitable, perhaps actively harmful occupations.

—Susan was much tempted to divulge the contents of Miss Crawford's letter to Mrs. Osborne, and beg her advice; already she found herself very ready to depend on the judicious, upright sense and quick understanding of this new friend; but a moment's consideration showed her that it would not do; she had no right to be disclosing Miss Crawford's plight to an outsider. She must make up her mind for herself as to the best course to follow.

Mrs. Osborne extracted her brother from the billiard-room, where the two men were not found to be playing billiards, quite a brief game having proved sufficient for Mr. Wadham's strength; they had been looking at maps and discussing ancient history, for Mr. Wadham, it seemed, was a scholar, a Latinist, with a decided bent for the pursuit and investigation of antiquities, and he had been quizzing Tom as to the likelihood of Roman remains being discovered on the Mansfield acres.

"I have been telling your cousin, Miss Price.' he cried eagerly, "that it is entirely probable that the great thoroughfare of Watling Street passed across his property—going from Ratae, which was Leicester, you know, to Verulameum—which of course was St. Albans. There is a very good chance that if we were to try an excavation *here*—" pointing to the estate map, "or *here*, we might come across the remains of a Roman posting station, or villa."

Tom, Susan could see, was quite charmed with the notion that his land might yield such an interesting discovery, and the two men were very well pleased with one another.—They bade each other a cordial farewell, and the parsonage pair walked off across the park.

Chapter 4

SOME HOURS OF REFLECTION MUST PASS BEFORE SUSAN FOUND
herself equal to the task of answering Mary Crawford's letter.
Among the difficulties to be faced was the fact that although Miss
Crawford, or Lady Ormiston, was probably not even aware that such
a person as Susan Price even existed in the world, yet she, Susan
Price, possessed a quite deep and extensive knowledge as to the
history of Mary Crawford.

How many times, when the two sisters were sitting sewing
together in the drawing-room at Mansfield, or picking roses in the
garden, or taking Pug for an airing in the shrubberies, had Fanny not
described those old days to Susan, telling the story of the summer
when the Crawfords came to Mansfield Parsonage; of how—
charming, good-natured, gifted as they were—yet they had
contrived to wreak havoc, and quite cut up the peace of the family
at the great house.

Henry and Mary Crawford had been brother and sister to Mrs.
Grant, wife to the incumbent at that time occupying the Parsonage.
Talented, lively, and attractive, they had been, ready to please and be
pleased; accustomed to polished London society, yet by no means

despising the pleasures of rural quietude. Yet their charm, based on mere easy good-nature, had concealed both calculating ambition and callous vanity. Their natures, fundamentally shallow, had been spoilt by the bad influence of an uncle who had brought them up, a man of gross ways and scandalous connections. Miss Crawford, with twenty thousand pounds of her own, had her heart set on a rich marriage; her brother Henry, endowed with a handsome competence, led the life of a man-about-town and was a selfish, thoughtless, flirt; untouched by any affection himself (save for his sister) he delighted to make young ladies fall in love with him, and, in this aim, his smiles, his lively conversation, and his caressing ways were universally successful. Maria and Julia, the two Bertram sisters, had both succumbed to his addresses, and both had, later, flung themselves into imprudent marriages in their distress and anger at the realisation that his intentions had never been serious towards either of them.

But then a strange thing had happened: the apparently heartless Henry Crawford had fallen deeply, sincerely, head over heels in love with the Bertram sisters' unassuming cousin Fanny, so much less handsome, less dowered, so much less accomplished or forthcoming than Julia and Maria, the acknowledged beauties of the neighbourhood. How it could have happened was hardly to be understood, yet so it was: the hitherto unconquerable, untouchable Henry Crawford was found to be pleading, with genuine, unaffected emotion, for the hand of Fanny Price.

"Why would you not have him, sister?" Susan always asked at this point. For in spite of his bad behaviour towards the Bertram sisters (and Susan, who could not like Julia Bertram, found no particular difficulty in pardoning someone who had used her slightingly) Henry Crawford, even as described by Fanny, who disapproved of him had—apart from the tendency to flirt—been endowed with every quality that could please. His looks were not handsome, but that was of little importance, since air and manner were so agreeable; he could talk entertainingly on every topic, was well educated, and had a great gift for acting, singing, and reading aloud; he was a skilful and intrepid horseman, a conscientious landlord, and was in many ways extremely kind-hearted, would go out of his road to do anybody a good turn.

"So why would you not have him, sister?" Susan would repeat. And Fanny always replied,

"Need you ask? Had he been endowed with every perfection of character as well as such superficial good qualities, I would not have had him; for I was deep in love with my cousin Edmund, and had been from a child.—And then, you know, there was the scandal regarding Maria; that, in the end, effectually sundered the two families. Poor Edmund! He felt it very much at the time, because of his attachment to Mary."

For that had been another complication. Mary Crawford, the sister, even more delightful than her brother—and without the heedless, vain propensity to flirt which impaired his character— Mary had been very much disposed to favour the suit of Edmund Bertram, although he was only a younger brother, and despite her ambition to marry money. And Edmund—to the unuttered, unutterable wretchedness of Fanny—Edmund had for a time fancied himself in love with the lively London beauty.

"She could play the harp so well, Susan—and her talk was so amusing—though sometimes, to my way of thinking, it bordered on impropriety. She could never resist making fun of the clergy; such levity used to pain poor Edmund sadly. The fact of his being in Holy

Orders, and of having only a younger brother's portion—these, I think, to her, were decided impediments to the match. Yet I think she did love him—as much as her shallow nature would allow—I think she would, in the end, have accepted him, if it had not been for the disaster of Maria."

Maria, now married to her rich and stupid husband, had met Henry Crawford again in London, and, still resentful at the way he had trifled with and then left her, had received him coldly and slightingly. His vanity was stung by this into making an attempt to win back her favour, and before he realised the danger he was courting, she had quitted her unloved husband and fled to him.

Good heaven! thought Susan at this point in her reflections. And is such a despoiler—such a libertine—to be received again, acknowledged again, within the precincts of Mansfield? Surely not! Tom would never allow it.

At that point it occurred to Susan that it was perhaps her duty to inform Tom as to the identity of the new tenants that he was, it seemed unwittingly, harbouring at the White House.

Tom, alone among the Bertram brothers and sisters, had not fallen prey to the fatal charm of the Crawford pair. Either because of better judgment, or insensibility, or lack of proximity, he had somehow been spared the general infection, and, his severe attack of fever happening to lay him low at the time when the rupture of Maria's marriage was taking place, he had by chance not been so painfully aware of the part played by the brother and sister. The name *Crawford* when mentioned to him by his agent had evidently not struck him.

Yes, Tom must be made aware who they were; it was undoubtedly Susan's duty to give him the information.—Yet, she felt, her paramount and primary duty was towards that poor invalid who had written to Fanny with such longing, with such affection and trust. At this very moment, perhaps—having not received the "No" which, she had asseverated, would be sufficient to turn her from her purpose— at this very moment she might be on her way hither; hoping to see her friends, perhaps, in a matter of hours.—Susan found that she could not bear such a notion, and summoned the butler.

"Baddeley, do you happen to know whether Mr. Tom's new tenants have yet arrived at the White House?"

She could be sure that in a village so small as Mansfield, such news would instantly be passed from mouth to mouth, and would be known to everybody in the place before sunset; the family at the great house would be the last to hear it, but their servants must be certain to have the information. And so it proved.

"Yes, miss, they came in a barouche from Northampton. The lady looked poorly enough, they say; very poorly indeed she looked, and was put to bed straight by her maid. Dr. Feltham is attending her. They are the same ones, miss, as was here some five or six years agone, before you was come to Mansfield, when old Dr. Grant was still at the Parsonage; 'twas the summer when Master Tom took a fancy for playacting and ordered a theatre to be builded in Master's business room. Lord, what a dust-up there was, to be sure, when Master—*old* Master that was—come back from furrin parts and found a platform built and fifty yard o' baize curtain in his study.— Yes, those at the White House be the self-same ones that used to be up here then, acting and singing and carrying on with Miss Maria and Miss Julia and Mr. Edmund. That Miss Crawford was a rare pretty lady. But 'tis said she's sadly changed now. The gentleman baint in any way altered, but the lady have lost her looks, they say."

"Thank you, Baddeley," said Susan, and, as soon as he had withdrawn, sat down to write her note.

"Dear Madam," she wrote, then crossed this out and substituted:

Dear Miss Crawford:

I have but now received your letter addressed to my sister Fanny and write in haste to apprise you of the sad news that my sister and brother-in-law are not in Mansfield at present. They have been obliged to sail for the West Indies on business relating to the recent death of my uncle, Sir Thomas Bertram. I took the liberty of opening your letter, having been instructed by my sister to inform all correspondents of her departure and her present whereabouts. I shall, of course, despatch your letter to her by the next sea-mail, but fear it may be at least sixteen weeks before you can expect to receive an answer from her. She and Mr. Bertram are not expected back before September at the earliest.

I am exceedingly sorry to be the means of conveying to you information which I know must cause you grief and disappointment.

I understand that you are not in good health, and at present may not be equal to society, so I will not venture to call upon you until I hear from you that such a visit would be acceptable; but I should be glad to do anything that lies within my power to remedy the misfortune of my sister's absence. Pray let me know if in any way I can be of service to you.

Yours etc.
Susan Price

Having despatched this by a servant, she went in search of Tom, only to learn that he had, two hours ago, gone off to Thornton Lacey, a small village at some distance from Mansfield in which he owned the living and an extensive stretch of property. He was not expected back for a day, perhaps for several days.—Tom was given to these sudden, unheralded departures, when the quiet and repose at Mansfield became too much for his impatient nature. During the time of his absence, therefore, nothing could be done.

Thought could hardly be avoided, however, and, during the customary evening's cribbage with Lady Bertram, while Susan mechanically counted, and reckoned up the score, and dealt her own and her aunt's cards, her mind ran continually on the new occupants of the White House.

What a contrast that poor woman must find, in the surroundings that she had recalled with such happiness: so many of those she had known previously no longer here; her own family departed from the Parsonage, besides the loss of Fanny, Edmund, Sir Thomas, Maria, and Mrs. Norris; all were gone, and Susan, who read extensively in Shakespeare, could not fail to be reminded of the line "Bare ruin'd choirs, where late the sweet birds sang."

How different, how much livelier, Mansfield must have been in those bygone days. Now there was only remaining Lady Bertram, who, easy and indolent even when young, brought by age to something not far from total vacancy, would hardly be valued as a companion, and Julia, on her fretful, fault-finding visits little more agreeable. Certainly there was Tom, but since, in the past, Miss Crawford had preferred his younger brother despite the difference in expectations, it was not to be supposed that she would have any greater wish for his company now; and in any case Susan could not imagine that loud-voiced, careless, insensitive Tom would be welcome in a chamber of sickness.

How is Miss Crawford to find entertainment here? she wondered, and then, with relief, remembered Mrs. Osborne. That lady would certainly bring cheer and comfort to a sickroom, and could be confidently expected in such a case to give her time with generosity.

Then, as well at the White House, there was Henry Crawford, and regarding the formation of *his* character Susan could not avoid considerable speculation. What kind of a man could he be, who would insensitively trifle with the affections of the Bertram ladies, yet fall genuinely, deeply in love with her quiet sister Fanny? What kind of man could beguile handsome, dashing Maria Bertram on to her ruin, yet remain during many years unattached and unmarried for the sake of her gentle cousin?

He was evidently a devoted brother, and that must stand in his favour; he sat by his sister's sick-bed, urging her, begging her not to die; he could therefore not be wholly deficient in heart and natural affections.—Susan did not deny to herself that she felt a curiosity to see him, though she feared there might be impropriety in her doing so. It was certain that he could never be invited to Mansfield; the betrayer of Maria Bertram could never be received there. Yet still Susan could not help wondering what Mr. Crawford was like.

Then, with a sudden start, she recollected that in fact she *had* met him, long ago, at the time when he had been eagerly prosecuting his suit of her sister Fanny. Fanny, reared among her cousins at Mansfield Park from the age of ten, had, when she was eighteen, returned to her family in Portsmouth for a visit of several months' duration. And Mr. Crawford, not able to bear the lack of her company for so long a period, had come down to Portsmouth to stay at the Crown; he had called at the Price home and had accompanied Fanny and Susan, then aged fourteen, on a walk round the Dockyard with their father; and on a subsequent fine Sunday had joined the Price family in their weekly promenade on the ramparts. Delving in her memory, Susan began to recall him with a fair degree of accuracy: a black-haired man, not handsome—no, he certainly was not that—yet well built, gentlemanlike, with a lively countenance and a very pleasing address. Even to the fourteen-year-old Susan he had taken pains to make himself agreeable, instead of plainly wishing her elsewhere, as a more vulgar or ill-natured suitor might have done.

Her conclusion, after all this pondering, was that he must be an interesting man; not unblemished as to character, but perhaps with sufficient better qualities as to make him capable of redemption. —Years had passed, after all, since the summer when he had flirted so dangerously with the Bertram sisters; years during which he had lived a steadier, simpler and more tranquil life on the estate in Norfolk. (Susan had ascertained by reference to the gazetteer in the library that Everingham lay remote from all towns on a stretch of the coast beyond King's Lynn.) He must, by now, be greatly matured, improved, less volatile, less tempted to flirtation or flattery, altogether steadier and more deserving of regard. It would, in course, be very disappointing for him to arrive at Mansfield and discover that the people in whom he must feel most interest had departed on a six-months' journey; yet, on consideration, perhaps this was no bad thing. To be meeting again the woman he had loved and who had preferred another man, to be meeting his successful rival—this *must* be productive of pain and chagrin. He might be relieved to find them gone. Perhaps indeed he had been dreading the encounter.

And Susan here applauded the unselfishness of a brother who, to give his sister comfort, would venture into a society where he might anticipate such pain, where he might, too, very probably be received with coldness and repudiation.

To say that Susan intended to seek the company of Mr. Crawford would be to assert a very unlikely thing; yet she had settled it with herself that she should not go out of her way to avoid an encounter; no, she should certainly not do that. It must be of particular interest to meet a man who had felt such deep, such sustained and overmastering love for her sister Fanny as to abjure any thought of ever marrying. Fondly attached as Susan was to her sister, this must be Henry Crawford's warmest recommendation to her: already she felt that she could entertain a sisterly regard for him.

Having discussed her state of mind to this degree, it was, naturally, a cause of no little dissatisfaction to learn from Baddeley, next morning, that the gentleman, his sister having been established at the White House, had left again almost immediately.

Later in the morning, however, a note arrived from the sister; a note brief, shaky as to orthography, suggesting all too clearly the infirmity of the writer, but warm and sincere in expressions of gratitude and a wish to meet the sister of her dear friend.

Already the air of this place does me good! In a very few days, I am persuaded I shall be able to leave my chamber and come downstairs; then I shall look forward eagerly to hearing everything that you can tell me about your dear, dear sister and all her doings. My brother, who, alas, had to depart on business, asked to be remembered to you; he says that he recalls a very pleasant walk on the battlements of Southsea, many years ago, when you were no more than a charming child.

Yours etc.

Here was gratification! and in the intervals of assisting Lady Bertram to write a few replies to the notes of condolence that still came trickling in, as her elderly and distant acquaintance learned of the death of Sir Thomas, Susan was able to enjoy the idea that she had been remembered, and pleasantly, by a man who up till this day had been no more than a name to her, but was now an object of decided interest.—She was very often thinking of him. She could not put him out of her mind.

The occupation of letter-writing was presently broken off by the arrival of Mr. Wadham, who had called to leave a pamphlet on Roman excavations for Tom Bertram, and, Tom being from home, was persuaded to stay and make his acquaintance with Lady Bertram. His quiet voice and gentle manners exerted an immediately favourable impression on that lady, and she listened very placidly to his conversation about the Mansfield parishioners and inquiries as to their families, sometimes, in her own way, sleepily responding.

"Is he so?—did she do that?—I was not aware of it—I do not know one of those children from another—he is a very good sort of man I believe—I have not been there—very well—pray do as you think best, Mr. Wadham—I always leave those matters to Sir Thomas, or to my son Edmund."

Mr. Wadham probably quitted the house not much wiser than he had come, in regard to the villagers, but with a generous donation from Lady Bertram towards the Poor Basket, and with *carte blanche* to act as he chose in relief of the needy and chastisement of sinners, were any to be found in such a contented parish.

At the conclusion of his visit Lady Bertram declared that she would take her rest early, as after so much exertion she found herself somewhat languid and heavy; Susan therefore accepted an invitation from Mr. Wadham to ride across the park with him in his barouche. He was going on, he said, to make the acquaintance of some outlying farmers but he knew that his sister would be happy to see Miss Price and he could drop her at the Parsonage. This exactly fell in with Susan's wish to tell Mrs. Osborne about the invalid at the White House, and ask for her counsel and assistance in mitigating the newcomer's lonely lot.

—She found that as a newsbearer she had been anticipated by the butcher's boy giving the information to the Parsonage cook that there was a sad sick lady at the White House who took nothing but beef tea and toast gruel. Mrs. Osborne had already been deliberating with herself whether she should not immediately call on the new arrival and offer her services; she listened with great interest to all Susan had to tell about Lady Ormiston or Miss Crawford.

The name *Crawford* struck her at once, and she inquired, "Did you not say, my dear, that the lady had been brought here by her brother?"

"Yes, ma'am, Mr. Henry Crawford. He escorted her here and has now left again."

"Henry Crawford. Gracious me!—Yes, of course it must be the same. How very curious. Henry Crawford—well, well—I fear he was a much-maligned man."

"Dear ma'am, what *can* you mean?"

"In a way—" looking consideringly at Susan "the tale is hardly fit for your ears, young as you are. Yet, since you are in all probability to meet the sister—and since your own sister Fanny was in some way concerned—perhaps I had best tell you, if only to clear the poor gentleman's reputation of an undeserved slur, which, so far as I know, he has borne unprotestingly."

Her curiosity naturally whetted to an extreme degree by these remarks, Susan could only gaze at Mrs. Osborne wide-eyed. That lady continued: "I heard the tale myself from Mrs. Norris, before her strength had completely declined, you know; she would be talking for ever about her niece, and the rights and wrongs of the business. Mrs. Norris, of course, thought nothing too good for her niece and felt that she had received a most undeserved rebuff. Well! Maria, it seemed, had a violent partiality for this Henry Crawford; nevertheless she committed the supreme folly of marrying another man, a man of far greater fortune who commanded neither her affection nor her respect. It seemed that Mr. Crawford had not recip-rocated Maria's feelings; yet she must have had hopes of him for when, wearied out by impatience and incompatibility, she finally left her husband, it was to Mr. Crawford that she turned. But he, according to Mrs. Norris, rejected her wholly, baldly informing her that he did not love her, had never loved her, that he loved another; in short, he turned her from his door."

"Good heavens, ma'am! Are you sure of this?"

"As sure as a person may be; for Mrs. Norris, in her eagerness to dissociate her niece from the slur of adultery, showed me letters—a letter from Maria to Crawford, still urging him, still beseeching him to relent; and his to her, even more adamant in refusal, enclosing her own note and requesting that he be spared the harassment of further correspondence."

"Where *was* she then? Whither had she gone?"

"She was staying with her sister. Mrs. Norris gave me to understand that, at the same time as the elder sister had rashly quitted her husband's roof, the younger one, who at that time was visiting friends in London, had eloped with the man whom she subsequently married."

"*What?*" cried Susan, to whom this came as utterly unheard-of and most startling news. That Julia Yates—now so high, at least in her own esteem, so well-conducted, such a pattern of worthy, frugal, impeccable respectability—could once have been so recklessly imprudent as to elope, was quite astonishing, hardly to be credited.

"Oh, I fancy it was all quickly hushed up and smoothed over; the young couple went to Gretna Green and married, and her father was then persuaded to receive them. Maria, apparently, had staid with them as far as Stamford, still in hopes that Crawford might be brought to change his mind. When he would not, in fury and bitterness of spirit, she determined that as *her* good name was irrevocably lost, she would take good care to blacken *his,* and would prevent him from marrying the woman he really loved. She therefore wrote her father that she was under Mr. Crawford's protection, and let it be thought that he was to blame for the rupture of her marriage."

"Perhaps," Susan said doubtingly, "he was at least *partly* to blame;

at least, so I have always been given to understand by my sister. He was a sad flirt, Fanny told me."

"More than probably there was blame on both sides; it is generally so in these cases where young people have behaved imprudently and allowed their feelings to run ahead of their judgment. I daresay the gentleman had encouraged hopes which he had no intention of fulfilling. But then *she* had committed the far worse sin of marrying a man whom she did not love; marrying him for the sake of money and position."

"So—good heavens—poor thing, she was punished heavily enough for the mere commission of an imprudent marriage. If it is true that she did not go off with Mr. Crawford—if she quitted her husband alone—what occasion was there for her to live in such disgrace and seclusion? Why could she not return to her father's house? It seems to me that she had damned herself, all to no purpose."

"Pride, Miss Price: pride and anger made her adhere to her resolve, once she had told her tale, to stand by her course. She wished Crawford to suffer; and she could not bear it to be known that he had absolutely repulsed her. She told me once, furthermore, in a mood of reckless bitterness, that anything would be better than returning to Mansfield 'to be lectured by Sir Thomas and preached at by Edmund and despised by the neighbours who had admired her before.' Life with an aunt who doatd on her, even in remote and confined circumstances, was greatly to be preferred. 'At least here I am independent and can do as I choose,' she told me. It gives me pain to suggest that she was merely waiting for the demise of her aunt, but one could not help suspecting such to be the case. Maria is a person of high spirit and strong passions—not to be guided by the advice of others. It did not trouble her that, by pretending to be worse than she was, she had caused her father inexpressible pain. 'He thinks me abandoned to vice; let him continue to think so,' she asserted. 'I would have had Crawford if I could; my father is right enough there. If the sin were in *resolution,* not *commission,* I have sinned. And now I care nothing what is thought about me!'"

Thunderstruck, aghast at these revelations of destructive passion and thwarted love, Susan could only sit silent, pondering over the story.

"And so poor Mr. Crawford has suffered all these years undeservedly—has borne the reputation of a seducer when he had done nothing? I wonder he would make no attempt to clear his name."

"Perhaps, like Maria, he did not care; having lost the woman he loved, he was not interested in mere vindication."

Again Susan sat silent, thinking of Mr. Crawford, who had never married, but lived ever since on his property in Norfolk, shooting his coverts and taking care of his tenants, remembering Fanny.

"Well, my child," said Mrs. Osborne cheerfully, "you look mighty grave, and so you should! It is a moral tale indeed! Do not marry for money, do not engage in flirtation with young men, do not attempt to revenge yourself by blackening another's name."

"I am not like to do any of those things," replied Susan smiling. "Fortunately for me, Mansfield contains none of the needful ingredients. There is nobody to flirt with, no rich suitor begging for my hand, and not a soul on whom I wish to be revenged at present.— I wonder," she added musingly, almost to herself, "what my cousin Maria will do now? In London?"

"Oh—very likely she will meet with no worse fate than many another whose first essay into matrimony has been disastrous—she will set forward on a second attempt, and may next time, with more experience and more reasonable hopes, achieve greater success. My brother Frank would scold, to hear me talk thus, but so it is; many a second marriage, when the parties are of more rational age and peaceable temper, has a firmer basis and promises better than one scrambled together amid the ardours and fervours of hot-headed youth and blind first love."

"Then you yourself, ma'am—" ventured Susan, greatly daring, "would *you* think it desirable to embark on a second marriage?"

Mrs. Osborne laughed heartily.

"Ah—" shaking her head "you have properly caught me there! No, my dear—never! Having been so fortunate as to achieve perfect felicity in one of those hot-headed young first marriages I have just been decrying—I forget whether it was a week or ten days between our first meeting and the marriage ceremony—I would never be so rash as to venture upon a second. But—good gracious—there is the church clock striking noon. We have gossiped away the entire morning."

Several of the ensuing days were fine enough to permit Lady Bertram to sit out on the terrace in the shade, languidly calling out a few directions to the gardeners, while Susan picked flowers for the drawing-room and little Mary set out her dolls on the flagstones and wrapped them in coverlids of leaves.

All were thus peacefully employed one morning when Tom came riding back from Thornton Lacey, looking hot and out of humour; at the same moment Julia Yates's chariot rolled to a halt in front of the house, and Julia alighted from it, accompanied by her children and her sister-in-law.

Susan always experienced a slight sinking of the spirit at the advent of Miss Yates. That young lady had brought to a fine art the quelling of pretension—or what she held to be pretension—in persons from classes of society lower than her own; as an earl's daughter, she naturally felt herself the equal of anybody in the kingdom, and higher than most. A Susan Price, coming from a shabby naval household in Portsmouth, her father no more than a lieutenant of Marines, her grandfather heaven knows what, must naturally come quite beneath Miss Yates's notice. Consequently if Susan happened to cross Charlotte's line of vision she generally contrived to remove her gaze elsewhere; and if Miss Price should for any reason address her, she would give a slight start, as if her thoughts had to be summoned back from an unimaginable distance, and emit a kind of languid gasp of surprise. "Oh—did you say something, Miss Price? I did not quite catch—"

Julia, when away from her sister-in-law, could be meddlesome, interfering, and captious enough, but was not wholly inaccessible to reason. When in the company of Miss Yates, however, Julia was accustomed to follow her style and turns of talk and to imitate her fashion of ignoring Susan, or—if Susan were to be noticed—treating her in a haughty and slighting manner, as though her very existence were a matter of question.

Lady Bertram, of course, observed nothing of this, and liked Miss Yates very well, only complaining that she talked too quick and that her voice was so soft that none of her remarks could be heard.

Susan bore with the bad manners of her cousin, and her cousin's sister-in-law as good-naturedly and philosophically as she could, going about her usual occupations in their presence, answering when addressed, which was seldom, and, in general, speaking as little as possible and keeping herself in the background.

On the present occasion, however, this policy proved impracticable.

Tom, having handed over his horse to a groom, came striding round the corner of the house with no very amiable expression on his countenance, addressed a few perfunctory greetings to his sister and Miss Yates, saluted his mother, and then directly approached Susan.

"Susan! How in the world does it come about that those disreputable people, the Crawfords, the ones who brought all the trouble, are established in the White House, and that you are in communication with them? What can you be thinking of? Are you gone quite mad?"

His remark brought a chorus of exclamation from the females on the terrace.

"The *Crawfords?* Why, Tom, you cannot mean those odious people—?" from Julia.

"Dear me! The Crawfords! How singular!" from Miss Yates; and even Lady Bertram, who had been dozing, opened her eyes and murmured plaintively, "Pray, what is the matter, Tom? What is it that has happened?"

Susan remained silent for a moment, from a wish to collect her thoughts, while all eyes were turned upon her. Then she said,

"As to how the arrangement came to be made in the first place, Tom, your own agent must know that better than I. It was Claypole, your attorney, who managed the business and chose the tenants—"

"Yes; and I shall soon say something pretty sharp to *that* gentleman, if he can take care of my business no better than to be installing such people—the very last one would wish to have about the place. But how comes it, Susan, that you have positively been engaging in correspondence with them—going behind all our backs in this secret, independent, self-regarding manner? Your position here is hardly such as to justify such liberties!" With even greater indignation he went on, "I was riding through the village just now when up comes Mrs. Osborne to me, she having just stept out of the White House. 'Ah, Sir Thomas,' says she to me—as if I were Jackson the carpenter, or *anybody*—'Ah, Sir Thomas, as I see you are on the way home, perhaps you would be good enough to convey a message to your cousin, Miss Price?' What could I do but comply, though with no very good grace—being employed as a common messenger, in *such* a way, by such a person, is not just in my style—on such a hot day, too, and when I was in haste to get home. 'Pray command me, ma'am,' I said however, 'what is it that you wished to ask Miss Price?' 'Oh it is not for myself,' she said then, as calmly as if it was nothing out of the ordinary, 'but I have just been visiting Lady Ormiston, Miss Crawford as she used to be, in the White House, and she asks me to send her compliments to Miss Price and say that she finds herself still very much pulled down by the effects of her journey, unable as yet to leave her bed; but nonetheless she will be very happy if Miss Price will do her the favour of calling in a few days, perhaps on Saturday!'"

"*What?*" cried Julia.

And Miss Yates remarked coolly, looking down her aquiline nose, "How very curious, to be sure! Decidedly encroaching!"

"The White House?" from Lady Bertram with a sigh. "Ah, how many years it seems since poor dear Mrs. Norris lived there.—Who are these people, Tom, that you do not seem quite pleased with?"

"Why, ma'am, the Crawfords, you must remember the Crawfords. Do not you recall that summer when they stayed at the Parsonage—when we were all acting a play, 'Lovers' Vows'—and my father was so displeased with us. And very rightly so, as it turned out, for resulting from the affair my brother Edmund was in a fair way to have his head turned by that Miss Crawford—if at the last moment his hopes had not been overset by—by the consequences of the brother Henry Crawford's behaviour towards my sister Maria—"

He stopt, frowning, as if what he had to say further were too bad to be communicated out in the open like this, even in the presence of none but family connections.—It may also have occurred to him that his sister Julia's marriage to Mr. Yates had been another consequence of the amateur theatricals, and the less said on *that* subject the better.

Susan felt an almost overmastering impatience to divulge what she had been told by Mrs. Osborne in Crawford's vindication and to Maria's detriment, but, with an effort, restrained herself. Firstly she could not feel that she had a right to make public what had been told her in semi-confidence—or not at least without first applying to the teller; and in the second place she felt tolerably certain that no one would believe her. Blood is thicker than water, and Maria was still the sister of Tom and Julia, though a disgraced and disowned one; why should they chuse to believe her more vindictive, revengeful, proud, stubborn, than they knew her to be already? Moreover the news that she had been spurned by the man whom everybody assumed to be her lover would be reducing her status as grand heroine of a melodrama to something infinitely less heroic; instead of being condemned, she must be despised, or pitied; and if a family is to have a black sheep, the scandal must naturally be preferred on a grand scale.

—Such thoughts as these passed through Susan's mind. Meanwhile Tom was saying to her in a very cutting manner,

"But *Miss Susan* here, who never met any of these persons before, since at that time she was dwelling in *Portsmouth*—" he made Portsmouth sound like a sink of vulgar depravity—"Miss Susan Price must needs get into communication with this precious pair; next, for all we know to the contrary, she will be issuing invitations for them to dine at the great house."

"Odious!" cried Julia again. "What *can* you have been thinking of, cousin?"

"Ah—decidedly odd," yawned Miss Yates. "Truly Gothick, indeed."

And even Lady Bertram said, "I am sure it was very bad. How came it, Susan, that you writ notes to these people that you had never met?"

Susan felt almost strangled with mortification and injustice; her throat was tight with tears, she flushed deeply and had much ado to command her countenance. She endeavoured to calm herself, however, took a deep breath, and when she was in tolerable control of her voice replied,

"You have a wrong notion of the circumstances, Aunt Bertram, Cousin Tom."

Towards Julia and her sister-in-law she did not look. "The first communication, in this case, came from Miss Crawford and was addressed to my sister Fanny. Mrs. Osborne delivered it to me, as it had been taken to the Parsonage. Miss Crawford wrote most affectingly, and properly too as it seemed to me, claiming the bonds of old acquaintance, adducing her very severe indisposition as a cause, and—and asking to be received at Mansfield. How could I, in conscience, have refused her?—But in any case, refusal was out of my power, for the letter had been delayed on the way, and by the time it came into my hands, Miss Crawford was already installed at the White House. All I could do was to reply and inform her that my sister was not here at the present time."

"Humph!" said Tom. "Where is this letter?"

Susan raised her brows. "I have despatched it, naturally, to Fanny."

Tom said, after a moment's hesitation, "And why did you not obtain the advice of some older person—some person more closely connected with the family—before thus hurrying into action, extending what must be construed as a welcome to this woman?"

And to whom would you have me apply? Susan felt like answering hotly. To your mother—who has not an idea in her head unless it was put there by somebody else? To Julia—who cannot even manage her own children? (At this present, little Johnny and little Tommy were busily wreaking havoc in their grandmother's work-box, snipping her silks and thrusting her scissors into the earth.) To Miss Yates? She swallowed, checked a hot rejoinder, and was beginning, "You yourself were away at Thornton Lacey, cousin, and the poor lady's state of illness and anxious hope must command my first consideration—"

At this moment they all became aware that another person had joined the group. Mr. Wadham, the rector, had been standing hesitantly at the foot of the steps—for how long, nobody there quite knew—evidently feeling considerable scruple at intruding on what was plainly a family discussion.

He now coughed politely and made his presence known.

"Ahem! Good morning, Lady Bertram; good morning, Sir Thomas. Miss Price. Your butler informed me that you were all out here taking the air; he proposed to announce me, but from where we stood I could see you, indeed, making such a pleasant party in the sunshine, so I ventured to set aside formality and take the liberty of joining you. What charming weather! I feel myself exceedingly fortunate that the spring is proving such a benign one. I daresay I may have counted a hundred clumps of primroses in Mansfield Lane."

He kept his gaze upon Lady Bertram during the greater part of this speech which seemed designed by its length to give the disputants time to recollect themselves and cool down; but one quick sympathetic glance directed at poor Susan's flushed countenance assured her that he must have heard a great deal of the foregoing discussion, that he understood and felt for her in her position; nay, even admired her for what she had done. Immediately her sense of injustice and misusage was lightened; she began to feel more comfortable; if but *one* other person felt she had acted rightly, the burden of family disapproval was nothing to bear. And such a one! Mr. Wadham was a kind, an intelligent, a discerning man; and a most agreeable one too. Not unamused, Susan observed with what a sharpening of interest Julia and Miss Yates were inspecting the newcomer, approving his gentlemanlike air, his easy, friendly manner, and his prepossessing countenance, as Tom introduced him. Lady Bertram, who had taken a calm liking to Mr. Wadham on his previous visit, quite brightened up, and issued an invitation to him and his sister to come and eat luncheon at the great house whenever they chose.

After a little general conversation Mr. Wadham produced the object of his visit, a paragraph cut from a newspaper which he thought must be of interest to Sir Thomas, for it related the discovery of a Roman pavement in a not-too-far-distant village.

Tom read it eagerly and exclaimed, "I have quite come round to your opinion, sir! I was talking to my tenant at Thornton Lacey and he agrees. I believe we should stand a very fair chance of discovering Roman remains either at Stanby cross-roads or by Easton copse. Why do we not make up a party, an excursion to go and inspect those places, to see which, on closer examination, appears the better subject for excavation?"

"Oh yes!" exclaimed Julia, clapping her hands. "An excursion! We can all go in carriages and take a picnic. It will be delightful, a *fête champêtre;* we shall wear bonnets—shall we not, Charlotte?— and Johnny and Tommy can bring trowels and dig to their hearts' content, and Mr. Wadham shall tell us all about the Romans. What could be more charming?"

"I am at your service," said Mr. Wadham, "whenever you care to chuse a day."

"But will not such an exertion be rather too much for you, sir?" said Susan.

He gave her a very kind look, as he answered, "I find myself so greatly improved in health, Miss Price, from two weeks spent in the invigorating air of Mansfield, that I can hardly believe *any* exertion, in these surroundings, would be too much.—Ah—excuse me." At this point Mr. Wadham stept aside, removed Lady Bertram's knife and scissors from the grasp of little Tommy and little Johnny respectively, they being on the point of slashing and gashing one another; gave the combatants each a light tap, gentle-looking but brisk enough to subdue for the moment their rampageous spirits and send them away in search of other diversion at the far end of the terrace; then he restored the misused implements (first cleaning them on his handkerchief) to their owner, who sighed and said, "Thank you, Mr. Wadham. I do not know how it is that little Johnny and little

Tommy are always so bad-behaved when their cousin, little Mary, is always so good."

Julia was silent from annoyance; and Susan, seizing the opportunity, said to Mr. Wadham, "I learn, sir, that your sister has been visiting Miss Crawford; she sent me a message to that effect by my cousin here—" glancing in the direction of Tom, who looked surly and displeased but could hardly break in. Susan went on, "Can you tell me how Mrs. Osborne found that lady? Is her illness of a very serious nature?"

"I am afraid it is," he replied, shaking his head. "My sister, who has a long experience of nursing the sick, from her many years at sea, is, I understand, not sanguine about the poor lady's chances of recovery. It is exceedingly sad, for she is still young, not above five-and-twenty, and, my sister tells me, of very prepossessing appearance and manner. Mrs. Osborne has taken a great liking to her, indeed, and is glad to be able to perform a good many services for the poor lady, who has only servants to care for her."

"What of her brother then?" said Tom rather gruffly. "Is he not there?"

Susan could see that Tom was looking decidedly uncomfortable. She guessed that he felt in grave danger of being put in the wrong, a state which nobody relishes, and Tom Bertram least of all, he being, at all times, quite certain of his own rightness.

"Mr. Crawford? No, having installed his sister he departed again. I collect, from what Mrs. Osborne told me, that he felt his presence in Mansfield might—might not be welcome. Ahem! On that head, Sir Thomas—might I crave the indulgence of a private word in your ear?"

So saying, Mr. Wadham took Tom's arm, in the most natural, friendly manner, and walked away with him down the terrace. Tom looked a little reluctant, and almost suspicious, as if he were afraid of being won over against his will, but he could not help liking Mr. Wadham very well, and feeling an instinctive respect for the older man's judgment.

They strolled together back and forth across a distant lawn, while Susan fetched some gingerbread for the little boys, who were now demanding attention, and Julia enthusiastically discussed with Miss Yates the plan for a picnic party to inspect the Roman sites.

"We may as well invite the Maddoxes—and the Olivers—and the Montforts—the larger such a party is, the better."

"No," here put in Miss Yates languidly. "Let us not invite the Maddoxes. They are sure to bring their cousin Miss Harley and I find her the most boring, insipid, affected girl that ever was. So vulgar, too; there is no bearing her company."

"True; you are right. It is a pity, though, because the Maddox brothers, on their own, are pleasant enough. It is too bad they always feel the necessity of including Miss Harley."

"Can you drop a hint to them not to do so?"

Even Julia looked doubtful at this.

"What are you girls about? What are you discussing?" here drowsily inquired Lady Bertram.

"A picnic, ma'am, to examine some Roman ruins that Mr. Wadham is wishful to excavate."

"Shall I be invited to take part? Shall I enjoy it?"

"Oh, no, ma'am!" her daughter hastily told her. "You would find it far too tiring and be fagged to death before you were halfway there. No, you shall stay at home, with Susan to look after you, and we shall tell you all about it when we come back."

"I daresay you are right, my love.—Susan, give me your arm to help me indoors. The sun grows too hot here. Julia, you will say all that is proper to Mr. Wadham for me. He is a very agreeable man—perfectly gentlemanlike and pleasant. I like him very well, and his sister also. Susan, where is my work-box? Ah, you have it, that is right."

Susan, though sorry not to see the last of Mr. Wadham, was delighted to escape from the company of Mrs. Yates and Charlotte. —And Mr. Wadham's long conversation with Tom bore most satisfactory fruit; whether he had put the case of Mr. Crawford in a juster light, or enlisted Tom's sympathy for the suffering sister, or both, the result was that Tom ceased to scold Susan for her dealings with the White House; indeed, she began to think Mr. Wadham must have said something quite decided in her praise, for she occasionally, thereafter, caught Tom's eye upon her in a look of wondering perplexity, and reconsideration.

Chapter 5

SINCE TOM, AT THE EXHORTATIONS OF MR. WADHAM, APPEARED to have withdrawn his objections to Susan's commencing an intimacy with Miss Crawford—or, at least, had ceased to give utterance to these objections—Susan waited her opportunity, and on a morning several days later, when Mrs. Osborne had come to sit with Lady Bertram, availed herself of the chance to walk across the park to the White House.

It was not without considerable trepidation that she rang the bell. So much had been said, so much hinted, so much suggested about the Crawford pair since Mary's letter for Fanny had first arrived, that Susan felt quite as if she were about to encounter the heroine of some wild melodrama. Tom seemed almost to regard Miss Crawford in the light of a *fata morgana,* a baneful influence, who had in the past nearly ensnared his brother Edmund, that most judicious and levelheaded of men, then, subsequently, bamboozled Ormiston into marrying her—and look what had been her effect on *him!* Locked up, witless and raving! It was true that Wadham, or at least Wadham's sister, seemed to have been charmed by the lady, but for Tom's part, he did not intend to go within a gunshot of the

White House; Miss Crawford need not think that she was going to wind *him* round her little finger.

Julia's opinion, loudly voiced on every visit to Mansfield, was even more adverse.—A shrewd, cold, heartless, scheming villainess. Mary Crawford had laid out her wiles to tempt Edmund into offering for her only when there was considerable reason to believe that Tom was dying of a consumption, so that Edmund would succeed to the title; such hopes having been proved baseless, the schemer had pretty soon sheered off. Later out of pure malice she had persuaded her brother Henry to attend a party at Miss Crawford's house where he would be bound to re-encounter the newly married Maria Bertram, and so had contributed to Maria's subsequent ruin.—There was nothing good to be said for Mary Crawford. Well, to be sure, she was quite entertaining, lively company, could talk well, and sing well, and play the harp.

"But *we* know that lively talk and facile accomplishments are not the principal object and ambition of a woman who claims to have taste and intelligence—do we not, my dear Charlotte?"

"Ah—certainly," drawled Charlotte—who might well be grateful for such a conclusion, since she was signally deficient both in liveliness of conversation and diversity of accomplishments.

To the maid who answered the bell, Susan gave her name and the message that she should be happy to converse with Miss Crawford, but only if that lady felt perfectly equal to the visit.— After a short interval she was invited to step upstairs and enter the sick chamber.

Susan's first impression was: How wonderfully elegant! For Miss Crawford lay against a pile of pillows, diaphanously enwrapped in a book-muslin bed gown, a chambray gauze shift, and a French net nightcap. The room was light, for the window had a southerly aspect, overlooking Mansfield Park, and the curtains had been drawn back, admitting all the air possible. The invalid's bed was placed so that she might command a view out of the window, and a chair had been drawn up beside it.

Hesitant in the doorway, Susan recollected with alarm that here was a lady of fashion, such as she had never encountered in her life before: somebody accustomed to move with ease and enjoyment among the chief of London society. What topic of conversation can I possibly find that will interest her? was an immediate, and panic-stricken reaction.

"My dear Miss Price—or no, I intend to call you Susan. You do not object? I feel already on such terms of intimacy with you that I hope we may dispense with the preliminary formalities. Please be seated. But chuse another chair if that one is not to your liking. Chairs in rented houses are always shockingly uncomfortable—oh, pray excuse me! I had forgot for the moment that the house belongs to your cousin. His chairs must, of course, be above reproach, and you are not to be blamed for them."

Susan, laughing in spite of herself, disclaimed any objections as to the chair and sat down on it. Her second impression, the elegance of invalid attire once put by, was of harrowing thinness and plainness. Wretched woman! How could anybody ever have said that she was beautiful? Why, she looked like a starving pauper—like a sheeted ghost!

Miss Crawford's face, which must once have been charming in shape and outline, was now nothing but skin and bone; two sparkling dark eyes looked out of shadowy sockets, and her bewitchingly shaped mouth was indented between two deep creases of pain.—But as soon as she spoke the painful impression was lightened by the warmth of her manner, by the way she seemed able to laugh at herself and at her own predicament.

"Was there ever anything so ridiculous as that I should cumber my poor brother with the burden of fetching me all the way to Mansfield on a wild-goose chase, to find the two people I looked to see were not here, nor like to be? All my life I have been continually committing such helter-skelter follies; indeed, as I look back on it, my whole life itself appears to have been nothing but a wild-goose chase. Only, what *was* the wild goose, I wonder? Does everybody have a wild goose? Do you have one, Miss Price—Susan, rather? I plan to call you Susan because already I feel like a sister towards you. In the old days it was my fond hope to address our dear Fanny as Sister; that hope, alas, was never to be fulfilled; yet somehow I have never managed to get myself out of the habit. I still think of her as a sister. And therefore, my dear Susan, *you* must accept me as one too. Do you have any other sisters? I seem to recall Fanny speaking of another, a younger one—Belinda, Betty?"

"It is Betsey, ma'am—I am amazed that you should remember!"

"Mary—you must call me Mary! How old is Betsey?"

"She is only nine."

"And brothers? I remember charming William, who became a lieutenant through my uncle the admiral's good offices. How has he fared?"

Susan explained that William, last heard of in the Mediterranean, was hoping soon to be promoted captain; then she was led on to tell the fortunes of Sam, now a midshipman, Tom and Charles, still in naval school at Portsmouth, John, a clerk in a public office in London, of whom nothing had been heard for several years; and Richard, a lieutenant aboard an East Indiaman.

"Such a fine family!" sighed Miss Crawford. "And yet I daresay they gave your mother trouble and anxiety enough in their time. But now they can be a source of unmixed gratification—lucky, lucky woman! Whereas I, childless and fated to remain so, can do no more than take an interest in the young families of my friends. But now tell me about Fanny—she has two children, I understand. What are their ages?"

"The baby, William, is but a few months; Fanny has taken him with her."

"Well-a-day, was that prudent? And yet I can sympathise; she would not wish to be parted from her lastborn. And the other?"

'The little girl is three; she remains at Mansfield; if you are well enough, another day, and would care for it, I could bring her to visit you. Her name is Mary. She is an excellent little thing, with a great look of both her parents—"

Susan paused, her heart wrung with pity, for at this point she observed Miss Crawford slip a cambric handkerchief out of her reticule and unaffectedly, though inconspicuously, touch away a couple of tears from her eyes.—They were indubitably tears; Susan had seen them sparkle on her dark lashes. And when, after a moment, she spoke, her voice was somewhat hoarsened.

"*Mary?* Fanny and Edmund called their daughter *Mary?*"

Susan hesitated. It had not occurred to her hitherto that there might be any connection between Mary Crawford and the naming of Fanny's little girl. Moreover, even now, she could not have positively vouched for there being such a connection; in fact—if the truth were told—it seemed to her in the highest degree improbable. Much likelier was it that the child had been named after yet another sister in the Price family, coming between Susan and Betsey in age, who had died at the age of seven. She too had been named Mary, an endearing little creature of whom Fanny, before she left Portsmouth for Mansfield, had been particularly fond.—Yet perhaps there had been an ambiguity—perhaps Edmund had some say in the naming? In any case there would be no object in rudely disabusing, dashing down the invalid's grateful, touched, spontaneous impulse of affection; surely such sentiments must be raising and doing her good? A faint colour had come into her face, she was not quite so waxen pale as when Susan first entered the room.

"The little girl was christened Mary Frances; the *Frances* is after my mother." Susan contented herself with saying.

"I shall be enchanted to meet her; you must bring her very soon. Already I feel as if I were her godmother. Now inform me as to the rest of the family: Lady Bertram, I collect, is still the same—dreamy, good-natured, never troubling to exert herself for anybody by so much as the shift of a finger, am I right?"

Susan smiled. "Yes; my aunt does not change."

"And you, I am persuaded, care for her with the same ineffable sweetness and patience that, seen in Fanny, when that duty was hers, caused my brother to fall head over heels in love with her."

"Oh no," said Susan seriously, "I am by no means so patient as Fanny; indeed there are many occasions, with my aunt or with my cousin Julia, when I am very close to losing my self-restraint."

"And yet you seldom do. Ha! Now I can see Fanny in you; at first I did not detect the likeness; you are taller, more striking in looks and colour; but now I do. You are Fanny, but a more forceful Fanny. And, to tell truth, from what I recall of Lady Bertram, if you *were* occasionally to stamp and scream and throw her embroidery frame out of the window, you would retain my entire sympathy and give her no more than her desert."

"Oh no! Poor lady! I am often very sorry for her. Her life is so inexpressibly tedious."

"She made it so herself," retorted Mary Crawford. "As we all do. She has made her bed and must lie upon it—and hers is a more comfortable bed than many.—But you spoke of Julia—how is she? She married that ranting man, I recall—Yates; does she rub along with him tolerably well?"

"So I believe. They seem to spend as little time as possible in one another's company; he is much occupied with sport or fishing, and Julia comes over to Mansfield as often as she is able. They have her sister-in-law, Lord Arncliffe's youngest daughter, living with them."

"Charlotte Yates; a detestable girl; I remember encountering her in London," said Mary Crawford instantly. "And I can tell from your expression that you have an equal detestation of Julia, but are too good-hearted, or too circumspect, to reveal it. You need not be afraid, though! I am no betrayer of secrets; you may look on me, if you will, as your mother-confessor."

She smiled at Susan, who thought in astonishment, Why, how could I have considered her to be plain? She is quite beautiful!

"And Tom? What of him? He is *Sir Thomas,* now. How does he support the honour? With some trouble, I would surmise; he will never be the man his father was. He will never have Sir Thomas's principles or abilities. Poor dull Tom, his mind distracted between his horses and his gambling debts."

To Susan's own surprise she heard herself replying, "Tom is finding it hard at first, ma'am; suddenly to become head of the family, with all the cares and responsibilities that state incurs, cannot in course be easy or comfortable, and so he is learning. Tom has been used to lead such a carefree life that the many burdens chafe him sorely and he takes them, perhaps, with undue seriousness; also he sincerely misses and mourns my uncle. Yet I believe that in time he may become as upright and conscientious a landowner as Sir Thomas. The will is there, if not the experience."

Mary Crawford eyed her narrowly. "He has a sincere and unprejudiced advocate in his cousin Susan, I can see; or perhaps you *are* prejudiced? Perhaps you entertain for him a warmer sentiment than mere cousinly regard?"

"No indeed!" cried Susan hastily. "You greatly mistake there, I assure you! To tell the truth, Tom and I are usually at loggerheads; I was the *little cousin Sue* for too long to be acceptable to him now as a companion whose opinion on anything can be worth heeding."

"Aha! And so he tramples on you and sets you at naught. I can remember, all too well, how often Fanny was used to receive such treatment, and how indignant it made me on her behalf.—So Cousin Tom is a blockhead, and no doubt he will marry Charlotte Yates?"

"Oh, I hope not! I cannot bear to think of my poor aunt Bertram reduced to such companionship. Charlotte would use her so disagreeably, I am certain."

"How altruistic you are," Mary said, laughing. "You think only of your aunt. But what of yourself, in such circumstances?"

"Oh, I could not remain; I am quite sure she would never wish *me* to continue a member of her household. In such an event, I must remove to the Parsonage, where I could always be sure of a welcome from Fanny; only then, without me, I am afraid my poor aunt would fare hardly. But, in truth—although I know that Julia wishes the match—I fancy that Tom has other plans in view. He has shown interest in a Miss Harley—"

"Louisa? I believe I recall her," said Miss Crawford, who appeared to have an encyclopaedic memory. "An orphan of fair-sized fortune, parents defunct, who lives at Gresham Hill with some cousins named Maddox?"

"Yes, that is she."

"She was but sixteen when I came to Mansfield before—never stopped talking or laughing—a pleasant girl enough, not stupid, but a rattle. Charming looks, I concede: hair and skin fair and soft as an infant's, besides a pair of ingenuous blue eyes.—Yes, she would suit Tom Bertram well enough, and, I daresay, use his mother more kindly than Julia's candidate.—So much for Tom, then, we have settled *his* fortune. And what of yourself, my dear?"

"Of myself?"

"Come, come! Let us have no assumed coyness. You need not take on that demure air with me. Do not be telling me that, with your looks, and your advantages, and the background of Mansfield, you yet lack a suitor?"

"I am afraid that is the case," Susan was obliged to admit. "The life we lead here is so quiet, so retired—My aunt never going into society—"

"Monstrous! Outrageous tyranny! I ought to summon my brother at once, and instruct him to call in half a dozen bachelor friends. And yet," said Mary Crawford with a sigh, abandoning her sportive tone, "I do not know, after all, why I should be urging you into the arms of the male sex. They have brought *me* little enough pleasure or comfort; and, from what I can see of the lives of my friends, matrimony is a state to be shunned, rather than sought."

Susan at this could not help but recall the decidedly opposing views of Mrs. Osborne, so recently uttered. She murmured that lady's name.

"Mrs. Osborne? Ah, but *she* is a saint! Lucky the man who

captured *her* affections—he could hardly avoid becoming a saint likewise. And by the bye, that reminds me—does she not have a bachelor brother? Who is, no doubt, as delightful as his sister? Ha, you look conscious! Well, I will not tease; but I confess I have a great curiosity to meet this Frank Wadham; I hope he will soon come to pay me a pastoral visit. You might drop a hint.—But now, my dear Susan, now that we have become such confidential friends, I wish you to tell me everything, every foolish detail, every daily triviality concerning the lives and happinesses of our dear Fanny and Edmund. Do not be thinking it will distress me—" twinkling away another tear—"it is what I am come for. It is the breath of life. To hear about them, about their virtues and unselfishness, will do me more good than anything else in the world."

When Susan left the White House, at the end of a two hours' visit, she felt an inclination to walk slowly, not to retrace her way across the park at her usual rapid speed, for she had so much to ponder, to sigh over, to feel, to recall, of Miss Crawford's look, manner, observations, and expressions, that half a day, even a whole day, would hardly be sufficient to absorb all the crowded impressions gained in the course of the conversation.

To begin with, she could not avoid the inference that Miss Crawford was gravely ill. Her emaciation, her dry cracked lips, her frailty—above all, her whole demeanour, that of one thirstily, feverishly endeavouring to secure a moiety of nourishment from life before it might be too late—all these things suggested that her state admitted of little hope; that she herself entertained none. She never said: "When I see Fanny and Edmund, when they come back, I shall do such-and-such—" she did not delude herself. She had accepted the harsh truth that she must manage to subsist on Susan's reports of Fanny and Edmund; that the living realities must not be depended upon.

I will go to visit her every day that I can manage, Susan resolved then. I do not care a straw what Tom says, or what Julia thinks. I will contrive to see her as often as possible; and I am sure Mrs. Osborne will approve, and will help in making arrangements for Aunt Bertram.

The next consideration must be to write a letter to Fanny.

"You will be writing soon to your sister?" Mary Crawford had said wistfully as Susan rose to take her departure. "You will give her—and Edmund—my love, my dear love? You will explain that at present I find myself too weak to write—such debility makes me excessively impatient, when I remember the long, intimate, nonsensical scrawls I used to be dashing off to Fanny all the time—which she, I dare swear, hardly read through, dismissed as trivial, frivolous stuff; yet writing to her always did me good; I felt I had access to a fountain of value, of integrity, even if it seemed to have little effect upon me. Yes, the mere process of writing to her used to winnow out my thoughts and separate the chaff from the good grain. There! You see how the very thought of Fanny inculcates in me, a city girl born and bred, poetical and pastoral images!"

Writing to Fanny, then, must be an immediate, if painful task; depicting the gravity of Mary Crawford's condition, and urging a speedy reply. Susan sighed, thinking of the period of time which must elapse before that reply could be received. As she walked, her fingers fairly itched for the pen; she was impatient to commence without delay.

But, on arrival at the house she discovered that, for the time being, withdrawal to her private sanctuary in the East Room must reluctantly be postponed; since, besides Mrs. Osborne, good-naturedly sitting with Lady Bertram and instructing her in the mysteries of carpet-work, other callers had arrived: Julia and Miss Yates were there, as well as Mrs. Maddox from Gresham Hill and her niece Miss Harley.

Observing all this company, Susan gave swift instructions to Baddeley, and a collation of cold meat, fruit, and cake was soon laid out on the large table for the refreshment of the party; also a message was despatched to Tom, reported to be inspecting his plantations at no great distance.—He returned after the visitors had been a short time assembled round the table; Susan could not help imagining Miss Crawford's ironic eye and satirical comments on the subse-quent behaviour of the party.

Susan's own entrance, of course, had been acknowledged by Mrs. Yates and Charlotte with the barest cool indifference; the hint of a curtsey, a half nod, was considered quite sufficient; and it was plain that the pair had been even less delighted to encounter Mrs. Maddox and Miss Harley; paying little heed to the ladies from Gresham Hill, Julia and her sister-in-law sat perfectly silent, or conversed with one another in low voices. Their ill-mannered silence, however, was concealed by the conversation of Mrs. Osborne, who, easy, cheerful, and well-bred, had been conducting a conversation about the beauties of the country with Mrs. Maddox and her niece. And Miss Harley, as always, talked enough for three; a good-humoured, exuberant, pretty girl, she smiled at all she saw, felt delight at all she experienced, and her chat bubbled out like water from a spring.

"Such delicious lambs on the way here—I do believe, Lady

Bertram, that the Mansfield lambs are the prettiest in the whole country. Their amusing capers had me laughing all the way—did they not, Aunt Catherine? Their long ears and long legs and little black faces are so bewitching, I do not see how anybody can ever have the heart to eat *spring lamb*—and yet, to be sure, spring lamb with mint sauce is so very good: Lord! what a great plateful I had last Sunday when it was served at my aunt's table. I fear I must be the most amazingly inconsistent creature in the whole of Northamptonshire—" laughing at her own folly—"but tell me, Lady Bertram, how does Pug go on? How old is he now? *Ten?* Good heaven, that is an age, indeed. He does not shew it; he looks very well. You remember me, do you not, you dear old Pug? Hark! how he snores at me, that means he likes me, does it not, Lady Bertram?"

"I do not know, my dear; in truth, he snores at everybody. It is his way of speaking, you know."

"Oh, I am quite sure he likes me"—stroking his nose; "I love him far better than my cousins' pointers, which are always underfoot, barking their heads off and muddying one's skirts; he is a dear, good old Pug, sitting like a graven image of the sopha, quiet and snoring, and his face is so delightfully black and wrinkled; I declare I love it better than anything else in the world, and if I were an artist I should paint a picture of it."

"And do you excel at drawing, Miss Harley?" kindly inquired Mrs. Osborne.

"Lord, bless you, no, ma'am! I could not draw so much as a chair without the lines being crooked. Charles and Frederick were for ever laughing at me when we were all children. Oh! how thankful I was to leave the schoolroom and know that I must never have my knuckles rapped again by cross old Miss Marchmont for blotting my copy-book and forgetting my recitation and ruling my lines askew. I believe one of the greatest pleasures of growing up is the knowledge that one need never be educated again. Do not you agree, Miss Price? Did you not detest being educated?"

"Oh, above everything," Susan told her, feeling, as she always did, quite charmed and disarmed by Miss Harley's inconsequentiality.

"But if you girls are not to be educated," said Mrs. Osborne, laughing heartily, "how in the world will you ever be able to instruct your own little ones when you have them?"

"Oh, very easily, ma'am; by hiring cross old Miss Marchmont to rap *their* knuckles and make them miserable. She is still about in the village at Gresham, you know, and I daresay will be happy to come and persecute them with her umbrella, and her snuff-box, and her tin of brimstone and treacle lozenges. How my heart used to sink as she stept into the schoolroom every morning, and how I used to cry, and pretend to have the stomach-ache or the tooth-ache, just to get out of lessons; I would sooner by far be put to bed with a poultice, or a dose of Gregory's Mixture; how many times have I not deceived dear Aunt Catherine here, who was always so good-natured and believed my tales of unspeakable agony. Ah! here now is Sir Thomas Bertram, come in from his coverts; tell me, Sir Thomas, do you not truly think that education is the most obnoxious process in the whole world?"

It seemed plain that Miss Harley's pearly teeth, her artless enjoyment of the company she was in, the ingenuousness with which she smiled up at Tom out of the corners of her long blue eyes, and the infantine fairness of her hair and complexion, could have persuaded him into agreement with any statement she made, however preposterous; he stood smiling down at her, displaying the most unfeigned admiration; and this irritated his sister and her companion so much that, very shortly after, they rose to take their leave, plainly hoping that Mrs. Maddox would follow their example.

"What, Julia, going already?" said Tom carelessly. "Surely you have but just now come?—Well, give my regards to Yates. When do we see him? He has not been to Mansfield this age. By the bye—" recollecting, "what about our party to view the Roman ruins? Have you mentioned that to Yates? Does he care to join us? And have you discussed the matter with your brother, Mrs. Osborne? Has he decided on which day he can best spare us for the excursion?"

Julia was excessively annoyed with her brother. To be fixing the arrangements for the excursion had, indeed, been her prime object in coming over to Mansfield; but she especially did *not* wish Miss Harley to be of the party, and had been proposing to go away without speaking of the project, rather than have it mentioned; for now, exactly what she did not wish to happen came about.

"What, are you to view some ruins?" cried out Louisa. "How charming! If there is one thing in the world that I doat upon rather than another, it is a ruin! I do hope, dear Sir Thomas, that I and my cousins and Aunt Catherine may be permitted to be of the party? Do you not doat on ruins, Miss Price? There is something so deliciously desolate about them."

"It is my painful task to inform you, Miss Harley," said Tom, "that no ruins are to be seen *as yet;* but still, with the help of Mr. Wadham, who is a great expert on Roman affairs, we may hope to unearth some."

"I do not mind! It is all the same! What a famous time we shall have! Perhaps we may discover a sword, or a suit of armour, or a skeleton! Oh I do so *hope* we discover a skeleton—it will be so very horrible! How we shall laugh! When is this party to take place, Sir Thomas?"

Mrs. Osborne was then again applied to, and a day in the following week suggested, discussed, and finally fixed upon. Tom stated his intention of inviting several other friends, the Olivers, the Montforts, the Stanleys, and the Howards; Mrs. Maddox was begged to notify her two sons of the scheme; and arrangements about carriages, who was to travel with whom, and what provisions were to be taken for the party's refreshment, all far too premature to be of any value, were generally canvassed.

Susan listened to all this with a detached mind, in the knowledge that, whoever went, she was certain not to be of the party.

Chapter 6

ON THE FOLLOWING DAY, SUSAN HAD THE RARE PLEASURE OF A letter from her brother William.

The Price children had never been burdened with undue attention from their mother. Mrs. Price, easy, indolent, not over-endowed with intelligence, resembled her sister Lady Bertram in all but fortune; given a life of wealth and comfort, she, too, would have been glad to lie on a sopha all day long and make fringe; but unfortunately she had married a lieutenant of Marines, a man of rough habits, irritable temper, and no ambition; the home in Portsmouth had always been small, crowded, disorderly, ill-kept, and uncomfortable. With little care from either parent, the children had been left to scramble themselves up into adulthood and knowledge of some profession as best they might.

Their uncle Sir Thomas Bertram had, indeed, probably done more for the young Prices than had their own father: arranging for William and Sam's entry into the Navy as midshipmen, finding a position for John as clerk in a City office, paying the fees of the younger boys at school, adopting Fanny at the age of ten, and Susan at fourteen. They had much cause to be grateful to their uncle.

Since there had been little warmth or affection spared to her children by the harassed Mrs. Price, they had naturally turned to each other in comradeship. Among the elder ones, William had always been Fanny's particular brother, until she was sent to Mansfield and he to sea; John and Susan, likewise, had been constant companions and friends. When John departed to London, Susan had missed him severely; the more so, as, having in him more than a touch of his mother's indolence, he did not trouble himself to write to Susan more than twice in three years, and had now not been heard from for some eighteen months.—She feared and suspected from this that he was not finding life easy in the metropolis. William, on the other hand, was an excellent correspondent, describing all kinds of adventures at sea in a simple but spirited manner which made his letters very entertaining. These were mostly directed to Fanny, yet latterly, since Susan had been resident at Mansfield, there was always a kind message and a remembrance to "Sister Sue"; and here, now, positively, was a letter addressed to herself, entirely her own property. "Since I know Fanny to be abroad I communicate with you, dear Sue," he wrote.

> Congratulate me! I have my Captaincy at last, and must post up to London next week for confirmation of it, and to receive my orders at the Admiralty. While I am there I must also find time to visit a lawyer, for my Uncle has been so good as to leave me £2000, which I had never expected, and am greatly Amazed and pleased at; I take it very kindly in him and only wish he himself were here to be thanked. The money will be of great assistance in furnishing me with the

necessary equipment, for a captain must be drest as befits his rank, and his cabin decently furnished, or his officers will never respect him. I should have been puzzled how to manage, even with £30 prize money from our last engagement; but now, thanks to my uncle's benevolence, I can spend with a liberal hand. Another piece of news is that I have a fortnight's leave of absence. While the *Heron* was refitting at Portsmouth I was able to see my mother and father, and the younger ones, so have no hesitation in soliciting to know if I may come and spend part of that time in Mansfield. Can you be so good as to inquire of my aunt and Cousin Tom if they have any objection to receive me? Of your own good wishes I have no fear . . . Yr affct Brother, William Price.

With what happiness did Susan, on receipt of this, inform Lady Bertram of William's success and inquire if his visit might be acceptable.

"William? Ah, to be sure, my sister Price's eldest boy. An industrious, good boy; I recall Sir Thomas was very taken with him when he came to Mansfield before. Sir Thomas said, I remember, that William had well repaid our benevolence towards him; as, indeed, he ought. I gave him 10L. when he went away . . . Indeed, it is not to be wondered at that he has done so well."

"Do you have any objection to my writing to say that he may come, ma'am?" Susan inquired, reflecting that Lady Bertram seemed to feel William's promotion to captain must be directly attributable to that ten pounds.

"No, my love, not the least in the world. But you had better also ask your cousin Tom. Tom is not quite pleased when matters are managed without reference to him."

Well aware of this, Susan had every intention of applying to Tom for his sanction.

She found him in the paddock, exercising a new young horse that he had recently acquired from an acquaintance, and intended training up to use in the hunting field during the following winter. Tom, observing Susan by the rail, turned and came cantering in her direction; the horse, which was only half broken, took exception to the appearance of Susan in her white dress, so much so, as to give several plunges, kick out, and caper about in a very excitable manner. Tom dismounted, handed him over to a groom, and came to inquire what his cousin wanted.

"Is not that horse rather vicious, Tom?" she asked impulsively. "I saw him take a great bite at John groom, and he lashed out at you too."

"Pho, pho, Cousin Sue! Confine yourself to what you know about, and leave management of my horses to me. There is not the least vice in the world about Pharaoh. He is full of tricks and spirits, playful, that is all. He will make a capital hunter by September, by which time I shall have made him know who is master, and cured him of his nonsense."

Discreetly, Susan said no more on the subject of Pharaoh, but handed Tom her brother's letter, and asked if he would have any objection to the proposed visit. Far from voicing any dissent, Tom's face lit up at the news.

"Cousin William? Capital! I have not seen him in an age. He is an excellent fellow. Promoted to captain? That is famous news; I daresay

he will very shortly be an admiral, and too high-up for us poor back-
ward folk at Mansfield. Do, cousin, by all means write to bid him here
for as long as he may care to remain.—And I tell you what—if he can
come to us before Thursday—he may make one on the excursion to
Stanby Cross and Easton Wood. William is a first-rate horseman; I
recall his mastering my black Sultan when he came here before; he can
ride my covert-hack and I will ride Pharaoh to the picnic."

Susan's face expressed some doubts as to the wisdom of this plan,
but she wisely held her peace. Tom went on, thinking aloud,

"By the bye, I have been considering that it would be no bad
thing if we were to have a ball at Mansfield; not a grand ball, you
know, nothing elaborate; that would not do, in the present circumstances; but that fellow Taylor whom I have taken on as second
woodman is a very fair fiddler, they tell me, and we could easily raise
five or six couple, just from the neighbourhood, you know, and
divert ourselves with a pleasant hop. What do you say, cousin? We
could summon the Olivers—and the Montforts; I daresay Wadham
and his sister would not object to come; *she* is rather old, to be sure,
but a clergyman may dance as well as any other body; and you and
I; and the Maddoxes, with Miss Harley—what do you say?"

Susan could not help being greatly engaged by the idea; she had
never in her life been to a ball, for although Tom sometimes attended
the Northampton Assemblies he had never thought to take her;
indeed her aunt could not have spared her; and, latterly, Sir Thomas
and Lady Bertram, preferring tranquillity and sobriety, had not
bestirred themselves to hold such entertainments at Mansfield. But
then she recollected, and said doubtingly,

"Do you think it would be quite right, cousin, so very soon after
my uncle's death?"

"Soon? You call it soon? Why, my father died in March, and here it is nearly June. Lord bless you! Where is the harm in that? To my way of thinking, three months is quite long enough to pay respect to the dead. I was as fond of my father as anyone may be, but one cannot be going about with a long face for ever."

"I think Mrs. Yates might object that it was rather soon."

"Julia? Oh, plague take her fidgets! She is always prosing on, these days, about propriety, about what is *done* and what is not *done;* all because she has that whey-faced Charlotte Yates staying with her. No one would believe that Julia herself once flung her bonnet over the moon.—I shall take no account of what *she* says. What a confounded nuisance that she need come to the dance; but I suppose she is certain to get wind of it, and will be pushing Miss Yates at me for a partner all the evening. *I* know, only too well, what she will be at. But she may spare her pains, for my intentions are quite other. I shall offer for Miss Harley in November; I would even do it now (for when one is engaged, all one's cares are over, and nobody else can be pestering one with wretched girls whose single ambition is to be off the shelf) but I do not wish to be tying myself up just yet, not until Christmas, at all events."

"Why Christmas?" inquired Susan, feeling a little indignant on Miss Harley's behalf, that Tom should be so confident as to her holding herself in readiness to have him the moment he might decide to drop the handkerchief.

"Why, one could not be entangling oneself in matrimony just at the very start of the hunting season! That would be the most devilish thing in the world! And yet, so it would turn out—by the time I had proposed, and she had accepted, and so on and so forth; we would be obliged to set forth on some abominable wedding-journey, to Paris or Florence or Rome, or some other wretched town abroad, just at the time when cub-hunting begins. It would be a great deal too bad, and quite puts one off the whole notion of marriage."

"You could propose today, marry in July, set out for Florence immediately, and be back at Mansfield in time for cub-hunting," suggested Susan.

"Now, cousin! Pray let me be managing my own affairs! Do not *you* be interfering—I have enough trouble of that kind with Julia. I do not wish to spend the whole summer meddling about with lists and troublesome business with settlements and all that marriage arrangements involve."

Susan rather wished that Mrs. Yates could have heard this conversation, that she might feel less confidence in her efforts to promote a match between Tom and Charlotte Yates. Almost every day at present, the weather continuing particularly fine and dry, Julia's barouche was at Mansfield, and she and Miss Yates would either be sitting with Lady Bertram or roaming about the gardens in search of Tom. The one advantage of this, for Susan, was that, from time to time, leaving Lady Bertram in the company of her daughter, she herself had more opportunity to slip across the park in order to visit Miss Crawford.

One objection to Tom's scheme for a ball which Susan had *not* voiced, for she knew it would only irritate him, was a feeling she entertained privately in her own heart and conscience, that it would be somehow wrong, almost wicked, for such an entertainment to be taking place, with all its gaieties and pleasures, when, so close at hand, somebody who would once have played a principal part and found particular enjoyment in those gaieties, was in such an evil case. It was cruel; the contrast was too cruel. She felt herself a traitor even to be thinking of satin sandals and spangled ribbons.

Occupied by these thoughts, she opened the wicket-gate that led directly from Mansfield Park into the garden of the White House; for, now that she was on terms of friendly intimacy with the household, she generally made use of this short cut.

In the garden, to her surprise, she discovered Mr. Wadham, putting together a nosegay of white pinks and sweet-williams.

"No," he said, smiling, as she greeted him, "no, Miss Price, you have not caught me stealing from my neighbour's garden; nor hoping to acquire the credit for presenting a posy garnered from the recipient's own borders; I have been sent out by the patient on this errand while Dr. Feltham examines her. Miss Crawford expressed a craving for the scent of clove-pinks, and bade me pick her some."

"I had not for one moment entertained such shocking suspicions of you," replied Susan, smiling also. "But tell me, how do you find Miss Crawford? Is she any better?"

"She declares her intention of coming downstairs next week; she wishes to be out of doors and sitting in the garden. But no," he said, sighing and shaking his head, "no, Miss Price, we must not deceive ourselves. I am too familiar with sick-beds to mistake; and so says Elinor also. Day by day she loses ground. It is terrible—particularly terrible—to see so rare, so radiant a spirit struggling, as she is, to fight against impending dissolution."

"Do you think she is struggling?" said Susan. "I do not. I believe her only wish is to see Fanny and Edmund again; if that deep, strong wish were granted, I believe she would say goodbye to life with an easy mind."

"And yet she takes such great interest in day-to-day matters! She questions me with such acuteness and vivacity about the events of the village—about my parishioners and their doings. And my sister Elinor tells the same story—Mary cannot hear enough of all she has to tell.— You stare, I daresay, to hear me refer to her as *Mary*, on such brief acquaintance, but she has invited me and Elinor to do so, and we have been spending such a deal of time with her that indeed we begin to feel like old friends; Elinor, I believe, passes the greater part of her day at the White House; she will run in before breakfast and again, I do not know how many times, during the following twelve hours."

"Mary Crawford is lucky to have you both," said Susan with tears in her eyes.

"She is lucky to have you, too, Miss Price; I know how little of your own time can be spared from Lady Bertram, and how much of that you contrive to pass at the White House. And I know in how strong a sisterly regard Mary holds you. It was a fortunate impulse that brought her to Mansfield. The journey may have hastened her bodily deterioration, but that I believe will have made no ultimate difference. Whereas the mental comfort that Mansfield affords her—even lacking the company of your sister and brother—the lightness of spirit that she has been gaining here, is, to me, a wonderful thing."

"I am very glad to hear that," said Susan. "It seemed such a heart-breaking disappointment that she should arrive to find them gone—almost unbearable. And I was afraid that had contributed to her—to the fact that she is not getting better.—I mind that so very much!" she exclaimed, unaffectedly wiping the tears from her eyes. "For I have become so truly fond of her. At first I believed that we could have nothing in common—she has been used to be so very fashionable and—and my sister, in the past, could not help thinking her somewhat *worldly*, with her mind fixed, perhaps, too much, on material advantage, and money, and high position. But I have found no such thing."

"I think, indeed, since she came to Mansfield, she has been changing daily," said Mr. Wadham. "She is an unique being, indeed; I am glad to have had the chance of meeting her."

His thin face, as he spoke these words, seemed quite irradiated; Susan could not help looking at him with a kind of anguish. Like an arrow in her heart formed the notion: he loves her! He loves Mary Crawford! What a terrible situation! She could say nothing further; her throat seemed closed with tears. In any case at this moment the doctor could be heard descending the stair, and they both turned indoors.

Dr. Feltham had nothing favourable to say. He had prescribed various medicines which might ease the symptoms but could do nothing to affect the ultimate issue.

"It depends on the patient's own resistance to the malady," was his verdict, "as to how long the matter may remain in doubt. Perhaps two months—perhaps less. Not having been long acquainted with the lady, nor being familiar with her constitution, I find it hard to judge."

"Do you think that her brother should be sent for?" said Mr. Wadham. "This point has been greatly exercising my sister's mind. Miss Crawford herself is much against his being summoned. 'It will be to frighten him, poor fellow,' she says. 'And why should I do that? I go on very well as I am; I have so many kind friends that I lack for nothing. If Henry is summoned he will be sure to come posting down to Northamptonshire in terror, believing me to be at death's door. Whereas it is no such thing!'—But what do you think, doctor? It would be dreadful for him if he were *not* summoned and—and the worst happened, and he was not here. We should reproach ourselves for ever. I understand that he is devotedly attached to his sister. Yet we do not want to alarm him unnecessarily."

"I believe you had best send for him," was the doctor's conclusion, after some thought. "It can do no harm; and it may help the patient to surmount this present increase in debility."

So saying he took his leave.

Mr. Wadham escorted Susan upstairs, but himself remained only a moment or two, to present his posy and deliver a message from his sister respecting a preparation of arrowroot which she proposed to bring later in the day. Then he, too, quitted the White House, giving Susan a brief, serious look as he left, which she received as an intimation that he or Mrs. Osborne would be undertaking the task of communicating with Henry Crawford.

"What a truly delightful man that is!" exclaimed Mary, when he had gone. "What a prize he will make for some lucky girl! What can you be thinking of, Susan, not to snap him up at once?"

But, seeing that Susan was not in harmony with this sportive vein, she at once relinquished it, and instead listened with the kindest, most unaffected interest, to the news from the great house, particularly the imminence of William's arrival.

"He was a dear, sweet fellow. She remembered him very well, and how delightfully happy he and Fanny were in one another's company. It did the heart good to see them. And then, too, Henry had liked him so well; had lent him a horse to go hunting, and thought very highly of his horsemanship.—They had traveled to London together. Henry had much to say afterwards of William's modest, sensible intelligence. And he was now to be a captain? Wonderful! And was coming to Mansfield? What a joy for Susan! Why, she had half a mind to write off directly to her own brother, and give him the happy intelligence. That might persuade him to come down and see William for himself, and spend a few days at Mansfield."

"Why not do that?" said Susan, to whom it occurred that this would relieve Mr. Wadham's scruples as to frightening Mr. Crawford unduly. "If you do not feel quite up to the task yourself, I shall be glad to write the letter at your dictation, you know, and you can sign your name at the foot. How would that be?"

"Oh, if I were not able to write my own letter, that would put my poor Henry in a sad fright! I have been accustomed to write him such screeds—to which he, of course, replies in a couple of succinct lines. 'Dear Mary, I am in receipt of yours. All at Everingham as usual. I shall be with you on the 11th. Yours sincerely.'"

But, after some persuasion, she was finally brought to permit Susan's writing the letter for her.

"I am forever sending off letters at my aunt's dictation," Susan pointed out. "To be doing so is nothing out of the common for me."

So the letter was written, and at the end Mary insisted on adding, "The receipt of this elegantly writ epistle you owe to the offices of a dear friend, already known to you from one encounter, long ago in the distant past; and I trust that your further acquaintance with her will be brought about by your compliance with my sisterly wish to see you here."

"There! That touch of mystery ought to be sufficient in itself to bring him hither. Now tell me of Tom, and the courtship of Miss Harley, and the unavailing efforts of Charlotte Yates. But first, why do you never bring my little namesake to visit me? Am I never to meet her?"

In reply to this plea, Susan divulged that she had, in fact, brought little Mary with her on the present occasion, but had left her playing in the garden, fearing that her presence might fatigue the patient.

"Fatigue? Quite the reverse! Pray send for her without delay!" cried Mary, all alight in a moment. "And tell Tranter to bring up some cakes and fruit. Dear little angel! I have been wearying to see her!"

Susan's fears, in fact, proved groundless, and the pair got on very happily together. Little Mary, at first somewhat awestruck in the presence of the grand lady swathed in muslins and gauzes, had her timorousness rapidly overcome by the lady's affable and cajoling manners. All Miss Crawford's toilet articles—of silver and ebony, ivory, tortoise-shell and crystal—proved also an irresistible attraction, and Susan, as she said, could very easily have left her niece there for hours together, solemnly gazing and touching and bringing things to show the lady in the bed, and carefully taking them away again.

"Fanny's child!" said Mary, with tears bright in her eyes. "Edmund's child! I recognise them both in every line of her features."

"I will bring her again tomorrow."

"The little love. Pray do so! Playing with her has restored my own childhood to me—my mind is now full of nothing but pot-hooks and samplers."

She kissed her hand to them both as they left the room.

Returned home, Susan despatched a message to the Parsonage to the effect that a letter need not be sent to Mr. Crawford, as his sister had written herself.

Chapter 7

FOR ONE REASON AND ANOTHER, THE EXCURSION TO STANBY Cross and Easton Wood had to be several times postponed: little Tommy Yates must be taken to Northampton for the extraction of an inflamed tooth, and was so poorly for several days thereafter that his fond mamma dare not leave his bedside; one of the Maddox carriage horses fell lame; Mr. Wadham's barouche had a cracked wheel; and then regrettable but necessary meetings of churchwardens and magistrates kept Tom and Mr. Wadham from the pursuit of pleasure for several days.

Meanwhile, however, the informal hop at Mansfield was in active preparation, and a night towards the end of the following week selected for the purpose. Tom rode about the neighbourhood issuing invitations; Lady Bertram was, as an afterthought, informed, but raised no objection, provided she was not required to take any active part in the business; Susan made the arrangements for the furniture to be removed and floors to be waxed; the violin-playing woodman was instructed to practise his country-dances and a companion who played the flute was presently discovered. Julia, of course, soon got wind of the scheme and came hurrying over to be affronted that she had not been consulted in the matter, complain that it was by far too soon after Sir Thomas's death to be undertaking any entertainment of the kind, to be won over by degrees as she reflected on the opportunity provided for Miss Yates and Tom getting onto closer terms; then to be annoyed all over again at the inclusion of the Maddoxes and Miss Harley among the guests; and to make a hundred and one suggestions for the betterment of Susan's arrangements.

"In the old days we *always* did such-and-such; balls at Mansfield were *never* conducted thus," was her constant cry.

"My sister Julia grows more infernally like Aunt Norris every week, I swear," grumbled Tom, throwing himself back in his armchair one evening when Julia had left them after an unusually lengthy discussion. "She is always so busy in other folk's affairs. She behaves as if everybody in the world had nothing to do but obey her whims and behests. It is the outside of enough. I begin to be quite sorry that she and Yates ever came to this neighbourhood. If only *she* had married Rushworth and settled twenty miles off at Sotherton, we should not be plagued with her advice and opinions a dozen times a week. By the bye, Susan," in a lower tone, glancing towards his mother who, across the room on her sopha, was just sinking into a gentle doze, "talking of Rushworth, and all that, I hear that my sister Maria is in a fair way to be married again."

"Indeed? From what quarter comes your information?"

"A fellow named Brooks with whom I was friendly at Oxford— now he is in Parliament and has a house in Hans Crescent; he writes me that the engagement is universally spoken of in London society, and it is thought that, all things considered, Maria has done remarkably well for herself."

"To whom is she engaged?"

"Ravenshaw is said to be the lucky man; let us hope that he can hold on to her tighter than poor Rushworth did."

"The Right Honourable Lord Ravenshaw who was used to be a cabinet minister?" asked Susan doubtingly.

"Yes, that is the fellow; I am quite surprised that you have heard of him, cousin! I did not know that you read the papers."

"Was there not some scandal connected with him? About fraudulent formation of companies, or something of that kind?"

"Oh, I daresay it was nothing so very bad; and in any case he got off with nothing worse than a lecture from the Lord Chief Justice, or some such thing; nothing could be proved against him, you know. And he is as rich as Croesus; Maria will be in velvet pelisses for life. That will just suit *her*."

"But did he not have to resign his cabinet post?"

"Well, what of that? She, after all, is no flawless saint. And he has his earldom."

"Then, he is so old! In his seventies, surely? Maria is only twenty-seven!"

"Come, come, cousin; I can see that, if you had your say, no one in the whole world would ever be married. You are too nice in your discriminations; I am sorry for the poor pretendant who ever comes asking for *your* hand. You will, for sure, be finding fault with everything about him."

He stopt suddenly, recalling that if Susan ever *should* take it into her head to accept an offer of marriage, the household at Mansfield would suffer the loss of an unpaid and exceedingly important factotum who managed the affairs of the whole establishment very capably, without noisy bustle, or putting herself forward, or giving offence to anybody.

—But then, with relief, he recollected that in November he intended proposing to Louisa Harley, and by December they should be married. Louisa was just such another good-natured creature; perhaps not quite such a clever manager as Susan, but *that,* she would learn in time; all that lacked was experience; and in sweetness of temper, docility, and happiness of disposition, she could not be faulted.

"Have you heard from my cousin William?" he kindly inquired. "When are we to expect him?"

"Tomorrow, Cousin Tom!" Susan's eyes shone at the thought. "He writes that he intends to travel down with a friend, Captain Sarton; and, so as not to be giving us any trouble, Captain Sarton intends putting up at the George."

"Pho, pho! There is no need for that. He may just as well stay here."

"William does not wish to presume on your kindness, cousin; and I think it very proper in him."

"Well, well; we shall see. If this Captain Sarton is a gentleman-like fellow—By the bye, Wadham said something to me of Henry Crawford's being sent for, or about to be sent for, because they were in anxiety over his sister's health; was that really thought to be necessary? She is not so gravely ill as all that, surely?"

Susan did not wish to be discussing Miss Crawford's state of health with Tom, who had resolutely refused to have any dealings with her or with the White House. She replied, simply,

"The lady herself sent a message asking her brother to come, because she had a wish for his company. And when *I,* who am perfectly well, consider how the prospect of *my* brother coming delights me, I cannot wonder at her doing so."

"I daresay it is nothing but a take-in," was Tom's uncharitable conclusion. "She has heard of the ball preparing at Mansfield and hopes, if Crawford is here, that he may find a means of getting himself invited."

Susan who, up to this point, had been quite in charity with her cousin, now found that she had to bite her tongue in order to prevent herself from giving a sharp rejoinder.

The joyful day arrived that was to bring William to his sister and witness the festivities at Mansfield. Susan could not help sighing, as she breakfasted, at the thought of Fanny and Edmund, so very far away; Fanny had many times told her of a highly momentous ball at Mansfield when she had danced with her cousin Edmund. "Though even in my happiness at his asking me I knew that nothing could come of it, for he was deep in love with Mary Crawford." How very differently matters had turned out! Far other than what the eighteen-year-old Fanny had expected!

During the day, despite the agitations caused by Tom's suddenly deciding that a pianoforte must be moved into the saloon although, so far as was known, nobody but Julia could play it, and the cook's expostulations about rout cakes, and Lady Bertram's having mislaid her favourite evening shawl, Susan contrived to find time for a visit to the White House.

She found Miss Crawford sitting downstairs, and very happy to be there, though Susan did not, in truth, think her sufficiently improved in aspect as to justify the removal; however, merely to be in a different room, and to be dressed in a gown with shoes upon her feet and her hair curled made her, she said, "feel a thousand times more like a human being."

Susan congratulated the invalid with all her heart, but was secretly grieved at the thin, lustreless hair, which must once have been so black and glossy; despite the maid's care and skill, it revealed all too plainly the real state of the case. Also she observed that Miss Crawford appeared to be in continual pain from her back; sit or recline as she might, it did not seem possible for her to be comfortable.

"There is a canvas back-rest up at the great house," Susan suddenly recalled. "It was made years ago for Tom when he had his fever, and he found it a great convenience. I am sure that Mrs. Whittemore will know where it is to be found. I will ask her to look it out and have it sent down to you."

"Oh, my dear Susan—pray do not be troubling yourself! It is like your thoughtful nature to suggest it. But you must have an infinite number of tasks to perform. Indeed I wonder at your charity in finding time to visit me today. Is this not the day of the ball?"

As she had done many times before, Susan marveled at the impossibility of keeping anything hidden in a village; she and Mr. Wadham and Mrs. Osborne had agreed on the advisability of with-holding the information from Miss Crawford, for fear of giving her pain by the contemplation of a festivity from which she must be excluded; and here she knew all about it!

"My maid Tranter heard it from the postman," she said, laughing at Susan's expression. "I collect that my kind friends believed me lacking in sufficient self-control not to scream and stamp and throw my plateful of gruel on the floor at news of a party to which I was not invited. But such is very far from the case, I assure you. I am looking forward with most eager expectation to your dancing every dance, my dear Susan; and I shall expect a minute-by-minute account, tomorrow, of all those dances, of what everybody wore, who sat by whom, who danced with whom, whether Tom Bertram proposed to Miss Harley or Miss Yates, and how Mr. Wadham acquitted himself as a dancer. And I shall require total accuracy of detail, you know, because Elinor Osborne will be giving me her report as well, with equal fidelity (except perhaps in the last particular) so that I shall be able to check her story against yours."

Laughing, Susan promised a faithful account.

"What shall you be wearing?" next inquired her friend; and then, sighing, "Ah, how long it seems since your sister came to see me on the very same errand, and I was able to persuade her that a necklace Henry had bought for her was really an old one of my own; was not that shocking! Otherwise she would never have accepted it. Dear, dear Fanny—what an age, a dreary age, it is since I have seen you!"

Then, shaking herself out of a brief, sad reverie, she once more inquired what Susan planned to wear for the party.

"Why—I have not a ball dress or anything very suitable for the purpose; my best gown is the one Sir Thomas gave me when I attended upon Fanny at her wedding. Happily it still fits me very well; I have grown a little since then but I contrived to let down the hem. In any case, this is not a grand party."

Miss Crawford threw up her eyes and hands. "Lord save us, these Bertrams are a pack of skinflints! Has it never occurred to your aunt that you might be requiring a new gown, or some money to buy one with? Or to your cousin Tom?"

"Oh, to be sure, if I said I required a gown, the money would be forthcoming; but then, you know, I never go anywhere in society, so it is not necessary."

"Gothick! Quite Gothick! I wonder they do not expect you to dress yourself in sackcloth and ashes. Well, I cannot give you a gown of mine, much though I should like to, for you are a head taller than I; but I have here a pretty trifle which I am in hopes you will accept—" and she withdrew from a folded tissue-paper an evening cap formed out of gold net.

"It is not new, I fear, nor, probably, in the latest fashion; but it has never been worn, and I greatly hope that you will do me the favour of taking and wearing it. With your long neck and your long almond-shaped brown eyes it will make you look precisely like Lucrezia Borgia, and that, you know, cannot but be of advantage to any young lady at a ball. Tom Bertram will probably be so over-whelmed that, forgetting Miss Yates and Miss Harley, he will propose to you on the spot."

"If it could achieve *that,* it must be the cap of Fortunatus!" said Susan, laughing. "And even if it were the latter it could not make me accept him. But, seriously—"

"Now! Now! I will not have any *'seriously'*—" affecting to cover her ears. "Pray accept the cap and let us have no more ado. *I* shall never wear such a piece of nonsense again, and I shall like to think of you dancing the Boulanger in it."

"Then I will wear it, and I thank you from the bottom of my heart for thinking of me.—Do you have tidings of your brother? Do you expect him?"

"Yes, and no. I have heard nothing, but that is Henry's way. In a day or so he will walk through the door without giving himself the trouble of being announced, and so I have the pleasure of continual expectation. *Your* brother, I understand, arrives today; you must be a very happy creature."

Susan's look, her smile, confirmed this conjecture. "And he brings with him a friend, a Captain Sarton, who will be staying at the George."

"What good fortune! So you will have a romantic stranger at the ball; every young lady will be struck by his piratical good looks and the enigmatic flash of his brilliant eye; but it will be at the sight of *you* that he starts with rapturous wonder and drops his gloves on the floor." Then, reflecting, "Sarton? Sarton? I believe my brother had a friend of that name; his father was once a crony of my uncle the admiral. I wonder if it may be the same? A very decent, unobjectionable, unassuming young man, as I recall. I shall be pleased to receive him if it be the same one."

Susan shortly thereafter took her leave and walked back to the great house in order to discuss with Tom for the fourth time the siting of the piano, to find Lady Bertram's shawl, and disabuse the cook of the notion that, since it was to be an impromptu party, three plates of rout cakes would be sufficient.

Dusk arrived, and with it William, alighting from a post-chaise in all the splendour of a new caped greatcoat and naval beard; Susan could hardly recognise him at first, he seemed so bronzed and altered in appearance: filled out, graver, stronger, and more manly. Yet underneath all this splendour and gravity was still the same eager, merry, friendly, round-faced William, as, after a half-hour's shyness and self-distrust, she soon discovered.

They had little time to talk together and exchange more than the first "Do you remember—?" and "When did we last—?" and "How is so-and-so?" before it was time to dress for dinner. Julia, her husband, and Miss Yates were of the party at that meal; John Yates addressed William very cordially, and the men were soon deep in discussion of horses, fishing, hunting, and William's accounts of scrambling parties ashore in the Peninsula; the visiting ladies treated William with cool incivility; as a simple captain must expect to be used who has only his pay and expectations of prize money; but he, in his enjoyment of being once more at Mansfield, and happy expectations of the forthcoming ball, did not observe this. The Wadhams were also there, and by them William was much better treated; Susan had the happiness of introducing him as "My brother, Captain Price"; Mrs. Osborne could talk to him of ships and naval acquaintances, and her bright eye and friendly smile denoted her approval of the new arrival; her brother, too, found topics in common, for William's ship had called, in the past, at ports in the East Indies with which Mr. Wadham was familiar. Susan, listening, glowed with pleasure at the lively intercourse that was going forward between her friends.

The half-hour after the meal was a period of ennui and impatience; Lady Bertram yawned in the drawing-room, Mrs. Yates and Charlotte talked together in low tones, and Mrs. Osborne exchanged unhappy impressions with Susan as to Mary Crawford's condition. Julia also took this opportunity of intimating her astonishment and disgust at Tom's idea that she might be willing to play the piano for the dancers, and her total lack of intention to do so.

"What! Thump away for an hour together while others dance? I thank you, no! It is a great pity that *you* never learned, Cousin Susan," with a sneer. "But I suppose pianos are hard to come by in Portsmouth."

Susan agreed calmly that this was the case, and added, "Moreover our house was so very small that I do not know where a piano could have been put, except, perhaps, in the cellar," which won her an amused glance from Mrs. Osborne.

The latter said, "I fear I cannot supply your deficiency, Miss Price, for a similar reason; none of my husband's cabins was ever large enough to admit of the introduction of a piano, or even a spinnet; consequently, after my marriage, all my musical propensities, which before that time were very strong, I assure you, had a sad stopper clapped on them, from which they never recovered."

Charlotte and Julia thereupon talked very perseveringly of music, and of composers and compositions and the importance of music in society and how essential it was for ladies to practise daily and keep up their proficiency, whether upon the pianoforte or the harp.

"What of your brother's friend, Miss Price?" inquired Mrs. Osborne. "Was I not given to understand that he traveled into Northamptonshire with a friend? Is he not to be of the party this evening?"

"Captain Sarton, yes; he did travel down with William and is putting up at the George. He wished not to be a trouble to our household, as he is a stranger to my aunt and cousin. But my cousin Tom very kindly sent a note to the George, inviting him to join us."

Sounds of carriages arriving and the peal of the doorbell now happily interrupted the conversation; guests began to assemble round the great fire in the saloon, and the scrape of a violin made Susan's feet tingle with the wish to be dancing.

A set was formed; Tom gave his sister and her friend mortal offence by leading off with Miss Harley instead of with Charlotte Yates; but the latter was invited to dance by the kindly Mr. Wadham, who talked to her very agreeably, so that her mortification was not visible to the public eye; William invited Susan to be his partner; Julia danced with one of the Maddox brothers, and the other Maddox danced with Miss Maria Stanley, one of two very good-humoured sensible sisters who lived not far away, were always available and happy to be invited on this sort of occasion, and occupied themselves, no one knew how, for the rest of the time.

Some while after the dancing had begun, Susan noticed an unfamiliar young man who had come into the room and was standing by Lady Bertram and Mrs. Osborne, who sat in the chaperon's chairs at the fire side, and apparently talking to them very entertainingly, to judge from their expressions. When the first dance was concluded, William introduced him to Susan; this, as she had inferred, was Captain Sarton, a thin dark man, not handsome, but with a look of great intelligence.—She had considerable pleasure in talking to him, soon found that they shared an interest in plays, poetry, and essays; in fine, she did not know when she had been so well entertained. Captain Sarton, as a consequence of a bullet in the kneecap sustained during his last engagement, was a trifle lame: "I should be happy to have the honour of dancing with you, Miss Price, but must warn you that I can do little more than shuffle about."

"That will be quite sufficient for me," said Susan, smiling, "but are you sure you ought to be doing so?"

"Come to a ball and not dance? Impossible!"

Meanwhile William, greatly taken with the cheerful rosy looks of Miss Harley, had invited her to be his partner for the next two dances; and as they were beside Susan and Captain Sarton in the set, Susan had a chance of overhearing their conversation, which was entirely about animals.

"Do you not doat upon dogs, Captain Price? I have an old spaniel that I believe is the nicest creature in the world—I love him beyond anything, he has such sad eyes and such drooping ears and such a faithful disposition; I do, truly, think that dogs are far superior to human beings, do you not agree?"

William did agree, and related the history of a pointer bitch whom he had smuggled on board the *Latona* when he was lieutenant aboard that ship, and what hunting parties she had graced on the Spanish coast and of her great fidelity and sagacity.

"And then there are horses and pigs—I am very partial to pigs, oh, there is such a charming family of little grunters just now on my uncle's farm—their snouts turn up so, and their tails are so curly, and their little eyelashes are so white that there is no resisting them! And calves, I adore calves, do not you? With their sweet breath, and soft noses, and liquid eyes. And ducks—I had a duck of my own for the longest time, she laid an egg every two days and had *such* a smile, but she was taken, in the end, by a fox, and I cried my eyes out for a week. Have you ever had a duck, Captain Price?"

No, William had not, but he had owned a parrot, purchased in the West Indies, and told Miss Harley many stories of its sayings and antics, at which she laughed immensely.

"Have you been up the Nile, Captain Price? Have you seen a crocodile? Or a camel? Or an elephant?"

Yes, William had seen all three, and was happy to describe these creatures.

Captain Sarton, smiling at Susan as he brought her a glass of orgeat when their two dances were concluded, said, "My friend William Price cannot fail to please. He is the most good-natured, sympathetic creature in the world. You are lucky to be in possession of such a brother, Miss Price."

"I am indeed. My sole complaint is that his profession must render our meetings so very infrequent."

"Then the pleasure must be all the greater when they do occur. I believe I should not be keeping you from his company."

Susan, however, had duties to Lady Bertram and the elder Miss Stanley; she had to see to the refreshment of the fiddler and his mate; and she had to pacify Julia, outraged because Tom had not yet once danced with Miss Yates.

"Now he is partnering one of those stupid Stanley girls, the younger; and what is *that* to the purpose? She has not a hundred a year of her own, and has never been beyond Kettering in her life."

"With such disadvantages, surely she deserves *some* recompense?" said Susan.

She found it hard to sympathise with Julia's displeasure; however, as the evening drew on, she found herself growing a trifle anxious about William, Miss Harley, and Tom; the two former seemed to have so *very* much to say to one another, they stood chattering for ever in corners, or sat talking their heads off on sophas, while William fanned Louisa with her own fan and she, pink-cheeked with pleasure, told him more and more about her tabby cat, her canary-bird, her mare Dulcinea, her black Leghorn hens, and a pet lamb she had once owned, which had died. William, it seemed, could not hear enough of her conversation. And Tom, it was plain, found the rapid progress of their friendship startling, and not particularly agreeable.

Lady Bertram presently declared her intention of retiring to bed, and Susan, returned from escorting her up to her maid Chapman, was surprised to discover the violin and flute replaced by the sound of the pianoforte, played with no little skill and spirit.—The executant proved to be Captain Sarton, who, smiling at Susan as he continued to play, said,

"This is a rare treat for me, Miss Price. Do not stop me! I told those two poor fellows they should rest for a while; since I can see that some of the party here intend to keep it up dancing into the small hours."

"If you are sure—? It is a great kindness."

"No kindness at all," he replied, rattling away at a great rate, "but my craftiness in contriving to give my knee a rest while acquiring the merit of being self-sacrificing, public-spirited, and a very good sort of fellow."

Mr. Wadham invited Susan to dance, and performed his part in a very graceful and gentlemanlike manner. His eyes told her that he admired her dress and the gold net which, as Miss Crawford had prophesied, did, on her dark hair, give her the look of an Italian lady in a painting.—She preferred his silent admiration to the more commonplace civilities of the Maddox brothers.

It was growing late when a slight commotion near the door attracted Susan's attention; she saw a servant go in quest of Captain Sarton, saw Sarton leave the instrument and walk into the hall; then she saw him return, apparently in search of somebody, and his eye lit upon herself. Guessing that she must be needed, she crossed the room to where he stood and asked if he were in need of assistance.

"It is not for myself, ma'am, but another gentleman, upon what seems to be an errand of mercy."

"An errand of mercy?"

Captain Sarton, who, perhaps from his experience in the service, had the ability to explain a complicated situation with brevity, said,

"While I was dining at the George this evening I encountered an old acquaintance from London days, also putting up there; and he, it seems, is come to solicit my aid in procuring a back-rest, which apparently was earlier promised for his sister, who is an invalid. She is in some pain, otherwise he would not dream of troubling you at so late an hour. His name is Crawford. He waits outside in the hall."

Chapter 8

SUSAN COULD NOT HAVE TOLD HERSELF EXACTLY WHAT SHE expected Mr. Henry Crawford to look like, but nonetheless he was a surprise to her. She had expected him, perhaps, to look older. Also, despite his sister's devoted attachment to him, and the vindication of his character by Mrs. Osborne, tales of his wickedness had, it seemed, lodged in her mind; she might have been imagining something in the nature of a Corsair, with black moustaches, or a scar, and flashing eyes, and a general air of dissipation and debauchery.—Her recollections from their previous and only meeting, when she had been only fourteen, were too scanty to form any basis for reasonable conjecture.

What she found, in place of her imaginings, was a very gentlemanlike, dark-haired man, not handsome, with a considerable air of weariness; dressed in stylish, if travel-stained, garments, clean-shaven, pale, and a good deal preoccupied. His look lightened at sight of her, however, and on Captain Sarton's introduction he said,

"Miss Price: I am a monster of inconsideration to be calling you out of a party at such an hour. But from my sister's report of you I have every confidence in your generosity—"

More than a little embarrassed, Susan stammered something in the way of greeting and apology, and then despatched a servant in search of the back-rest.

"I am thoroughly ashamed, Mr. Crawford, that it was not sent down before. Indeed, I was confident that it had been—but this has been a day of sixes and sevens, and I ought to have inquired to make certain that my order had been obeyed. It will be here in a moment. Have you a conveyance to carry it?"

"Thank you, yes, I drove up in my curricle. I am putting up at the George, in order not to over-strain my sister's house-hold.—Please tell me, Miss Price," he went on in a low, agitated voice, too absorbed in his own thoughts to stand upon ceremony, "tell me, how do you find my sister's state of health? I was never more shocked than when I saw her this evening; she seems so changed, even since I left her here. I looked to find her greatly improved from benefit of the country air; but the reverse appears to be the case. Do you not think so?"

Susan hesitated. She felt that somebody ought to tell the unfortunate Mr. Crawford what was probably the true state of the matter; but doubted if she, a mere bystander, unknown entirely to him, only recently acquainted with his sister, were the fit and proper person for such a disclosure. And this evening, surely, was far from being a suitable occasion: he, weary after a journey, distressed at first sight of his sister, and she in such pain; and the incongruous sound of music and dancing coming from the saloon; it was all very bad; morning would be a better time for what had to be said, and somebody else, preferably Mr. Wadham, or Mrs. Osborne, or the doctor, a more appropriate person to say it.

These feelings turning over in her mind, she attempted to prepare a short formal statement, some meaningless civility, to the effect that more time must be given, that the sudden warmth of the season, the dry weather, the over-excitement due to expectation of seeing her brother, his late arrival—that all these things must be taken into account, that progress in such cases must be expected to come slowly, etc., etc.

Intending to utter these platitudes, she looked into Mr. Crawford's eyes—he was not a tall man, they were much of a height—and found herself unable to give voice to any of them.

She said, "Your sister is happy, Mr. Crawford; of that you may be certain. I do believe she is as happy now as she has ever been. Is not that strange? How should I, a person who never knew her until a few weeks ago, be so sure of this? And yet I am. Now that you are come, I believe she has little more to wish for."

And still they were exchanging that long, candid look; as if they had been knowing each other for the past ten years.

The servant came hurrying with the canvas back-rest, and Mrs. Whittemore's apologies: there had been so much to do, with the rout cakes and the lemonade—she was sorry, very sorry indeed, that the leaner for the lady at the White House had been overlooked.

At the same moment, Tom walked out of the ballroom. He had left the dancers intending to go in search of William and Miss Harley, who, instead of dancing, had strayed out on to the terrace; Mrs. Maddox, Miss Harley's aunt, had invoked his good offices to find Louisa and persuade her to obey the dictates of propriety and return indoors—or, at the very least, to put on a shawl. At sight of the group in the hall, Tom checked, with a look of astonishment, then came slowly towards them.

"Crawford? I am not mistaken? How very—I am so—That is to say, how do you do?"

He seemed exceedingly embarrassed at the encounter. Susan could hardly be surprised. She herself felt that she had coloured to the roots of her hair. One of the several different mortifying thoughts that came to distress her was: How angry Tom will be that I should have dared to lend out the appliances of Mansfield to a stranger—and such an unwelcome stranger—without first asking his leave. She felt ready to sink through the floor.

But Tom, though he frowned at the back-rest in a puzzled manner, as it was carrying out to Mr. Crawford's curricle, did not seem inclined to make any inquiries about it.

The latter said quickly, "My dear Bertram. I have already been offering my apologies to Miss Price. I now do the same to you. It is infamous—unforgivable—to be breaking in on you at this hour. My sister's infirmity—the exigency of her condition—must be my excuse. I will now take my leave, and will do myself the honour of waiting on you at a more civilised hour tomorrow to reiterate my regrets."

He was turning away, about to leave, when Tom, appearing to recall their former friendly relation, or his duties as a host, exclaimed, "Stay—will you not come in?—will you not join us? My sister Julia—"

His voice failed, he looked at Crawford as if, for once, he found himself wholly at a loss. The latter smiled briefly and said, "Your sister Julia would not be at all delighted to see me. No, I thank you; I am in haste to return to *my* sister.—But it was kind in you to issue the invitation. I will bid you good night."

He stept quickly out through the open door and almost at once his horses could be heard departing at a rapid trot.

Julia chanced to pass through the hall at that moment, with a wrap on her arm.

"Was that the Miss Stanleys leaving?" she inquired.

Tom replied, "No, it was not any of the guests. It was Crawford, Henry Crawford."

"*Crawford?* That odious man? What in the world was *he* doing here? Hoping to spunge an invitation, I presume."

"No, he was not, Julia," said Tom wearily. Just then he looked so perplexed and despondent that Susan could find it in her heart to feel sorry for him.

To Julia, who still looked her inquiry, Susan said, "Mr. Crawford came here in order to borrow that old canvas back-rest which Christopher Jackson once made for Tom when he had the fever. His—Miss Crawford—is in great pain, and we—I thought that it might render her more comfortable."

At another time Julia might have seized on such an opportunity to expatiate on Susan's thoughtless encouragement of encroaching interlopers, unscrupulous use of Mansfield property, self-assertion, sneaking secretive behaviour, and general untrustworthiness and presumption; but Julia was feeling fairly satisfied with the way the evening had gone. True, Tom had not led off the ball, as he ought, with Miss Yates; but from that moment on his pursuit of Miss Harley had received such a severe check, such a bafflement, that Julia's own hopes now seemed in a much better way to be fulfilled. —And if William Price intended serious courtship of that ninny, Louisa Harley, they were welcome to each other! For Julia's part, she doubted whether William had a thousand pounds to his name, and if he ever rose above captain—wholly lacking in high friends or influence as he was—it would be little short of a miracle.

So she contented herself by saying, in a tone of haughty astonishment, "Tom's back-rest? Borrowed for Miss Crawford? I do not imagine we shall ever see *that* again," and passed on into the saloon.

It was not to be expected that the party would sit down in any very cordial spirits to breakfast next morning; all had retired late the night before, and there was a general air of lassitude, fatigue, and unwillingness to converse over the tea and coffee. Except, that is, for William, who had risen at seven, taken a turn through the gardens and coppices; had an excellent appetite and much to ask his cousin Tom about drainage, tillage, timber felling, and a host of related topics. His unimpaired cheerfulness and flow of spirits, his evident unawareness of having committed any fault, and the happy unconsciousness with which he consumed his cold ham and hot toast rendered it impossible for Tom to be bearing a grudge against him. The two cousins presently walked out into the sunshine and Tom was heard inviting William to come and inspect the paces of his newly acquired colt.

Presently in came Mr. Wadham and Mrs. Osborne to talk over the ball and show Lady Bertram a charade that Mr. Wadham had composed:

"My first is when my whole is heard,
My second sounds the traveler's rest,
My whole's a bird, and yet my third
Would drown its song and drench its nest."

"Dear me, Mr. Wadham, how very clever. I am certain that I shall never be able to guess what it can be. 'My whole's a bird'—good gracious—can it be a swan? A peacock? An eagle?"

Seeing that Lady Bertram would be comfortably entertained for hours by this puzzle, Susan slipped away to the White House to inquire whether the back-rest had at all helped to alleviate Miss Crawford's discomfort.

She found the brother and sister sitting in the sunny garden, the back-rest in position; and congratulated the sister very sincerely upon the improvement which this change must denote; indeed she did think Miss Crawford looking better, more animated, with a touch of colour in her cheeks and a livelier aspect.

After a few moments Henry rose and left them, saying that he believed his sister did better with only one caller at a time, and he would see to his horses at the George, take a turn about the village, and revive old memories.

"He has encountered an acquaintance at the George," said his sister. "Captain Sarton, your brother's traveling companion. But now, tell me about the ball: did your cousin Tom propose to Miss Harley? Were you much admired? I am able to inform you immediately that you have *one* admirer—my brother has not been so greatly struck since the last time he was in Florence and visited the Uffizi Palazzo— and that, let me tell you, was a long time ago! Seriously, he was greatly impressed by your appearance, and only feels it a great shame that you should be languishing here, unseen by the polite world, in the season of your chiefest youth and beauty. I tell him that you are playing a more essential role by keeping *me* cheerful and entertained; which he is prepared to accept, though with an ill grace.—In good earnest now, what do you think of Henry?" she went on, observing Susan to be not in the mood for banter. "Is he what you expected? Is he how you imagined your sister Fanny's lover?"

"No, not at all. Oh, how can I tell? I do not know. He seems very—very serious."

Susan found Miss Crawford's questions hard to answer; she spoke almost at random. Her friend, after giving her a long, acute look, said kindly, "You are fatigued after the evening's pleasures and difficulties. Never mind telling about them. They will keep. Some other time will do to tell me about how Miss Yates snubbed Captain Sarton, and how Julia found fault with the rout cakes."

Studying Miss Crawford, now that her brother was gone, Susan began to think the apparent improvement delusive; the colour, she suspected, was a touch of rouge, and the animation merely that brought on by the joy of his presence. She insisted stoutly, however, that she was better—much better—in a fair way to being quite well. Only her eyes betrayed her.

"The back-rest is an immense comfort. I am infinitely obliged to you for the thought of it. Chair backs are so hard and so vertical! And I am infinitely happy that you and Henry have met; it was one of my chiefest wishes, but I hardly dared hope that it might be fulfilled. All I have left to wish for now is Fanny's return."

Her self-mocking smile wrung Susan's heart.

"You did not bring little Mary to see me today? You thought I should be too occupied with Henry and should not want her. But you were wrong; quite wrong; I always want her, and she always does me good. Pray bring her again soon—tomorrow."

Susan promised to do so and went away shortly thereafter, not wishing, by her presence, to keep brother and sister apart. Besides, she had her own brother to seek out. She was deliberating in her mind how she could best hint to him that in wooing and pursuing Miss Harley so guilelessly—and without, presumably, any very serious intentions—he was doing a decided disservice to his cousin Tom; only, how to put this in such a way that it would effectively convince William? She could imagine him laughing and saying that Cousin Tom must look out for himself; if the young lady's affections were so easily beguiled away from her first suitor, then they could not have been so very strong to begin with. Such sisterly admonitions were not to be given immediately, however: on her return home Susan discovered that William had borrowed Tom's covert-hack and gone out riding with Captain Sarton; he did not reappear until dinnertime, when it was learned that the two friends had taken a turn round the countryside and incidentally called at Gresham Hill to inquire whether Miss Harley had been much fatigued by the exertions of the evening. There they had been most kindly received by Mrs. Maddox and invited to take a nuncheon. William brought messages that the lame horse was now better and that the Maddoxes would hold themselves in readiness at Tom's disposal whenever the scheme to uncover the Roman ruins should again be in train.

William himself, thus apprised of the plan, was all active enthusiasm; he had seen some capital Roman ruins himself, at Herculaneum and at Rome and that other place in Spain; those Romans were certainly devils of fellows for going about the world and leaving great ruins behind everywhere! What puzzled him was why they never seemed to build walls to their houses, but only those great draughty pillars and arches, with nothing to keep out the weather? But if there were Roman ruins to be found on Cousin Tom's property, he would be very happy to see them, and if they needed to be dug out, why, give him a spade, and he would dig; it would be famous fun.

Tom's own enthusiasm, which seemed to have diminished somewhat, was rekindled by this support; messages were sent about once more, and, the weather continuing favourable, the third day following was fixed upon for the scheme.

At such short notice the size of the party must, of necessity, be reduced; the Howards and Montforts had other engagements, Captain Sarton must return to London; but the Yateses declared their eagerness to come, and so did the Maddoxes; so did the Stanley sisters if any body could convey them; and Tom said that he already had a confirmation from Mr. Wadham that he would be happy to attend the group and could carry two extra persons in his barouche, which would account for the Stanley ladies and Susan.

Susan declared that she must stay with her aunt, who could not spare her. During the afternoon, however, she was surprised to receive a note from Mrs. Osborne. "My dear Miss Price: I am hoping that you will do me the favour of allowing me to remain with Lady Bertram while you join the picnic party. To tell you the truth—Roman ruins are no treat to me; I have seen countless examples of them at every Mediterranean port you care to mention. I shall far prefer to sit comfortably with your aunt in her drawing-room or under the shade of the arbour, while you are all grubbing about in the heat or eating chicken bones on your laps. And I feel that the party will benefit by the presence in person of the one who, I am very sure, will have made most of the arrangements. Yrs sincerely, Elinor Osborne."

How very kind in Mrs. Osborne! was Susan's natural reaction. She wishes me not to lose a whole day of William's company.

Going in search of her aunt in the arbour, Susan asked whether Lady Bertram would have any objection to the substitution. "Here is Mrs. Osborne, ma'am, offering to sit with you on Thursday while I go to the picnic. Would you mind this exchange?"

"Go to the picnic, my dear? But why should you do that? Has Tom suggested it? Does he wish you to be present? Does Julia? Do you wish it yourself?"

"Why—I do not suppose my cousins would be unwilling for me to go.—I could oversee the servants, you know, with the refreshments, and so on."

"You have never gone on such an excursion before."

"No, ma'am—but then, there has not been one."

"Oh dear—well—I do not know what to say. We had best ask Tom when he returns."

Tom, who came in presently, hot and tired from a day spent schooling his horse, had no objections to the inclusion of his cousin on the expedition. He felt that it was exceedingly kind of Mrs. Osborne to sacrifice her own pleasure—very disinterested and obliging indeed. To be sure, then Susan could keep an eye on the service of the nuncheon; there was something to be said for the plan. —Julia, on hearing about Susan's addition to the party, wholly disagreed. She saw no necessity for it at all; why could not Mrs. Osborne be minding her own business? What affair was it of hers?

"William may like his sister to be of the party," suggested Tom.

"He does not over-burden her with his society while he is in the house." replied Julia.

It was true that William, though a loving brother, did not propose to pass the major part of his day, as Susan must, of necessity, in the company of Lady Bertram. He found his aunt, who could not remember the difference between Malta and Majorca, a dead bore, and, though kind and civil always when he engaged her in conversation, spent no more time with her than was proper. He was happy to escort Susan about the village or anywhere else if she walked out; at other times he borrowed a rod from his cousin Tom and fished the stream which ran through the Mansfield woods; he also hired a horse from the George, because, he said, it was a shame to be always spunging on his cousin's stable. Thus mounted, he explored the country, and was absent from the house sometimes for several hours at a stretch.

✿

Thursday came, and though warm and still as the preceding days had been, carried with it something of sultry oppressiveness, which made Tom shake his head as he looked at the sky, and say,

"I wish we might have gone sooner. I wish we had gone when the scheme was first canvassed. I fear the weather is about to break; we shall be lucky if there is not a storm."

Susan hoped that Tom might be wrong. She herself had so many things to do, ensuring that her aunt's tapestry-work was in a fit state to be left to her own operations on it, arranging for the amusement of little Mary, who was considered too small to be of the party, and overseeing the carrying out of her and Tom's orders for the refreshment of the picnickers—which had been countermanded and altered so frequently by Julia that the servants were in a state of continual confusion—that she had little time left to be observing the sky.

"Did you wish the cart with the lunch to be driven to Easton or to Stanby, Tom? Here is Baddeley very perplexed, because he says he understood you to say Stanby Cross, but Mrs. Yates told him that you changed your mind and it was some other thing. And was it to be at noon, or at one o'clock?"

"I wish Julia would not find it necessary to meddle! Let her take care of those two ill-behaved brats, and leave me to manage my own business."

Despite these difficulties, and the melancholy prospect of William's departure on the following day, Susan could not help a feeling of eager pleasure, as, the final instructions given, the final arrangements agreed or disagreed, she stept into Mr. Wadham's barouche, taking the place of Mrs. Osborne who had gone up to Lady Bertram, and exchanged greetings with the Miss Stanleys, who were filled with equal enthusiasm.

"Such a charming plan for an outing—they had been on nutting parties, and bramble-picking parties, and sketching parties, but a *Roman* picnic was something quite out of the common, and sure to be the talk of the neighbourhood. Perhaps Mr. Wadham would discover a Roman bath—perhaps as a result of his investigations, Mansfield would be wholly changed, and presently rival the city of Bath as a fashionable watering-place."

Susan thought this unlikely, but was not wishful to argue. Since she had rarely traveled beyond the confines of Mansfield, save when it was necessary to escort her aunt to the dentist in Kettering, she found novelties and beauties to admire on every side, in the leafy copses, luxuriant hayfields, and ripening crops of summer; she would have preferred to sit silent, enjoying the unfamiliar scenes, but, since the good-hearted Stanley sisters were great talkers, felt it only civil to keep the conversation going.

"And was it true that Captain William Price had been riding over to Gresham Hill every day; that he was in earnest to make up a match with Miss Harley? So their cook had heard from the carrier, who had it from his sister, who was a dairy-woman at Gresham Hill farm. And was it true that Mr. Crawford, the brother of the sad sick lady at the White House, was about to take a lease of Stanwix Lodge? So said Mr. Knight the apothecary, who should know, for his brother, Mr. Sam Knight, was the clerk of the attorney who was to draw up the agreement."

Susan was unable to confirm either of these rumours; the first one made her decidedly uneasy, and she began to feel that, greatly though she would miss William's cheerful company, it was, on the whole, a fortunate circumstance that tomorrow would see the conclusion of his visit.

Tom and William, on horseback, soon overtook the carriage and drew on ahead, Tom calling back that he could not possibly ride alongside because Pharaoh was too fidgety.

"He needs a gallop to settle him down.'

Pharaoh did seem decidedly restive, tossing his head against the bit, and plunging across the road. The Miss Stanleys had heard that Sir Andrew Pickering, from whom Tom had purchased the colt, was glad to be rid of him because he was too ill-mannered to train. The anxiety which this information bred in Susan began, a little, to dull the pleasure of the outing; she knew that Tom had not ridden Pharaoh outside the training paddock before, and only hoped that the colt would behave himself during the day's varied activities.—She would be glad when they were safe home again.

It had been arranged that the Yateses and Maddoxes, who came from different directions, should meet the party from Mansfield at Stanby cross-roads. From that place a cart-track led to Easton copse; at that point it would probably be necessary for the company to dismount and proceed on foot.

The Maddox carriage was already there and waiting when Mr. Wadham pulled up his horses at the stone cross, and the Maddox brothers, on their horses, could be seen a quarter of a mile down the cart-track with Tom and William.

Mrs. Maddox and Miss Harley gave them cheerful greetings.

"Good day! Is it not sultry! Our friends and brothers are gone on ahead, and bade us inform you that we are to follow on foot: the lane is quite dry and not at all dirty underfoot, but too narrow for the carriages. Sir Thomas believes that Easton copse will be the pleasantest spot for lunch, since the trees will give us shade; so we may be inspecting its capabilities while we are eating our nuncheon. Perhaps, Mr. Wadham, you will not object to escort us forlorn ladies, who have all been deserted by our gallant cavaliers?"

Mr. Wadham declared himself happy to do so.

"I am wondering," said Susan, "whether I ought not to wait here for the Yateses; otherwise it is possible that they may not know which way we are gone. When I heard Julia discussing the rendezvous yesterday, with Tom, it sounded to me as if she had only an imperfect knowledge of this part of the country, and was not quite certain which place he was alluding to. And I cannot see any sign of their carriage."

All the party gazed around them. Stanby cross-roads lay at the height of a gentle eminence from which, in several directions, a considerable stretch of the country could be seen; but the view was not complete, for patches of woodland blocked off part of the scene. The road along which the Yates conveyance might be expected was not visible for more than half a mile along its length.

"Will they not guess, when they see the carriages, which way we are gone?"

"But there are two tracks here; and I am not quite confident that Julia understood Tom's intentions. They were disputing about the spot a great deal yesterday. Do you all go on," said Susan, "and I will remain here, sitting on the milestone, until I see them coming and can give them directions."

She was able, by perseverance, to overcome the various remonstrations against this scheme, as well as the offer of the friendly

Stanley sisters to remain with her, and soon had the pleasure of seeing the five others set off down the deep narrow lane without her. For Susan it was no hardship at all, but, on the contrary, a most unwonted treat, to sit alone in the midst of a warm summer land-scape and listen to no sound but the shrilling of larks overhead.

After fifteen minutes or so, she began, however, to be a little perturbed, and to wonder if the Yates party had been delayed, had been misdirected, had mistaken the time, the day, the road?

At last, much to her relief, she detected, in the distance, what looked tolerably like John Yates's claret-and-green chaise and pair; but, to her perplexity, it seemed to be headed in the wrong direction, going along a road that led sideways around the hill, instead of directly approaching the cross-roads. Susan attempted to attract the driver's attention by calling; she even climbed up on top of the mile-stone and waved her parasol, but apparently to no avail; the claret-and-green equipage proceeded on its way, out of sight beyond a patch of oak coppice.

Troubled by this, Susan wondered what she ought to do. Should she rejoin the vanguard of the party and inform them of this deviation by some of its members? Or remain here, trusting that the Yateses would presently become aware of their error, and turn back?

While she still hesitated, she observed, and guessed, that the latter possibility had come to pass: the claret-coloured coach was again to be seen, proceeding in the contrary direction. And, after another fifteen minutes, it came slowly towards her up the hill and drew to a halt by the cross.

"Hollo!" called John Yates, who was indeed the driver. "You are there, Miss Price? But you are all alone. Where are the rest of the party?"

In a moment the heads of Julia and Charlotte appeared protruding from the carriage windows. Both looked flushed and out of spirits. And from the inside of the carriage came the angry cries of the little boys, who appeared to be fighting a battle.

"So *here* you are, all the time!" exclaimed Julia, with a decidedly irritable note in her voice. "Well, *you* look cool and comfortable enough, to be sure—while we have been driving hither and thither over the hot countryside. Where are the others gone?"

"They went on along the track to Easton copse," replied Susan. "I remained here to give you the information. The lane is not wide enough for a carriage."

But here she was interrupted by John Yates, who cried out, "Pho, pho, what nonsense! Of course it is wide enough for any but a looby. It is wide enough for any man who can drive tolerably well. I will guarantee to get along there without so much as a single scratch on a panel."

His wife here coolly but absolutely disagreeing with his statement kindled him into an attempt at proving his boast; but he almost at once arrived at such an exceedingly narrow corner that he was obliged to dismount from the box and back his horses, slowly and with the greatest possible difficulty, all the way back to the milestone, where there was a gatepost to which they might be tethered. While this difficult manoeuvre was in process, Julia, growing impatient, had scrambled out of the carriage and over a stile in the hedgerow, exclaiming,

"Come, children! Come, Charlotte! As the lane is blocked by John's stupidity, we may as well walk alongside in the meadow. Besides, it is far pleasanter to walk upon grass; the lane is so dusty."

Charlotte and the two little boys followed, and were lost to view on the far side of the hedge.

Susan was wiser than to be reminding Mrs. Yates that the field in question was a hayfield, and that the farmer who hoped to reap the crop would not be best pleased to find it trampled over with footprints; she held her peace, and, as she had not been invited to join the Yates ladies, waited until Mr. Yates had made fast his carriage, and then quietly walked down the lane. John Yates, at a rapid stride, soon caught her up.

"Hey-day, Miss Price! Why in the world did Cousin Tom inform my wife that the quickest way to Stanby cross-roads was by Thornton Parva and Norman Bank? It was no such thing—took us four good miles out of our way. And then Julia would have it that we must go *round* the hill, not up it—she said Tom had told her so distinctly—we should be wandering yet, if we had not met a shepherd, who redirected us."

Susan, who had heard Tom and Julia disputing over the route, was well aware that he had told his sister no such thing; but there was no sense in adding fuel to the fire of everybody's annoyance. She replied peaceably that they must have mistaken one another's meaning.

"But it is of no consequence, as you are here now."

Farther along the lane they were rejoined by Julia and Charlotte and the little boys. One of the latter had fallen and cut his knee; and Miss Yates was in a state of angry distress and expostulation as she had been stung by nettles in the hedge, *very badly,* she said, on her ankles and on her arms.

"You should look for a dock-leaf and apply it to the stings," kindly advised Susan, beginning to feel a little sorry for poor Miss Yates, who was obviously quite unaccustomed to country walking. She had on a pair of blue nankeen half-boots, very elegant, but wholly unsuited to a rough scrambling excursion. Also, Susan suspected that they were too tight and pinched her feet. Her cheeks were flushed, her elaborate feathered hat was askew and her hair coming out of curl; she looked almost ready to cry with irritation and discomfort. But at Susan's friendly suggestion she turned away haughtily without being at the trouble of replying, as if the latter's proximity merely added to her numerous vexations.

"Pray, Charlotte, do not be making such a melodrama about a few nettle-stings," exclaimed Julia unsympathetically. "Little Johnny has been stung too, but he does not cry, do you, my angel?"

However as at this moment little Johnny scratched himself, attempting to pick a wild-rose, his roars quite drowned her question. Since Miss Yates continued to complain that her stings burned her like fire, Julia hastily pulled out a vinaigrette and applied a few drops to the afflicted parts of her children and sister-in-law.

They walked on along the lane, the children grumbling at the distance, Charlotte in continual uneasiness at the dust from the dry ground which was soiling her beautiful boots; every few yards she would stop and attempt to clean them on tufts of grass at the roadside.

Susan, who could now see some of the others in the distance, would have liked to walk on ahead, instead of proceeding at such a dawdling pace, but did not think it would be polite to do so.

At last they reached the little group who were waiting by a gate, in the shade of a fine thorn tree whose boughs were clustered thick with cascades of blossom now tarnished to a creamy gold hue.

Greetings were exchanged between Mrs. Maddox, the Stanleys, and the Yates ladies. Julia glanced discontentedly round for the men, then asked, "Where is Miss Harley? Was she not able to come?" in a livelier tone than she had yet employed.

"She walked on with Mr. Wadham into the grove, where the rest of the gentlemen are gone; we remained here in this delightful spot in order to direct you." replied Mrs. Maddox. "Shall we follow them now?"

Between the gateway and Easton copse, the small oak coppice which was their destination, lay a widish green meadow, grazed by a few far-distant sheep and cattle. Its surface was studded here and there by small boulders, and in the middle of the pasture a slight declivity, marked by tufts of reeds, suggested the presence of a bog or spring concealed in the grass.

Having passed through the gate the seven assorted persons and two children proceeded at varying speeds across the field; John Yates, followed by his two sons, whom he completely ignored, strode rapidly ahead, skirted the marshy area, and was soon out of sight among the trees.

Susan, Mrs. Maddox, and the Stanley sisters walked together after Yates in a loose group, taking care to avoid the marsh, the Stanleys pausing to pick cowslips, admire kingcups, and exclaim at the warmth of the day and the purple orchises to be seen here and there.

Mrs. Maddox engaged Susan in conversation with great civility, expressing her gratification that Miss Price had been able to form one of the party, as she knew it was not easy for the latter to leave Lady Bertram; but she was extremely pleased to have this chance of making Susan's better acquaintance.—What can she possibly mean by that? was Susan's first alarmed thought, but she responded with warmth, and soon felt herself to be on very comfortable terms with the older lady.

Behind them she could hear Charlotte talking in a tone of whining complaint to Julia.

"*Very* peculiar treatment, to leave the ladies to make their own way across a field—not at all what she was accustomed to—gnats and midges were biting her to distraction—where in the world were the gentlemen—did not at all like the look of those shocking great bulls, or oxen, or whatever the beasts were over there—rocks everywhere, one was in continual danger of turning one's ankle—odiously warm day—not in the very least what she had been expecting."

Susan could hear Julia's reply.

"My dear Charlotte, I fully enter into some of your feelings. It was very wrong—very ungentlemanly and discourteous for the men to abandon us in this abrupt manner.—But we can guess whom we have to thank for *that*. Mansfield is far, very far, these days, from being governed by the spirit that prevailed when *I* was a child. No: I fear it is now ruled by inconsideration, impropriety, and vulgar pushfulness. These things are bad, very bad. Those who do not in any way deserve it, claim attention, while real merit goes neglected.— No, I regret that Mansfield is shockingly far from being what it once was. The *place* may be there, the stones and bricks, the trees and meadows, but any feeling of calm and good breeding has wholly vanished.—However I have not lost all hope of its redemption, and restoration to what it once was; all that it lacks is a right-thinking guide, a mentor, a leader in taste and propriety, to correct the many faults, and give a different direction to the notions and manners of those who live there."

Miss Yates sniffed, and paused to disengage a prickle from her skirts, but made no audible reply.

During this speech, Susan quickened her pace a little, in order to pass out of earshot. She observed that Mrs. Maddox did likewise, and the latter gave her a quick, friendly smile, as if she, too, having heard the preceding remarks, deplored them but felt they deserved no comment.

They had just arrived at the copse, and were moving with gratitude into the welcome shade of the trees, when they heard a slight shriek from behind them, and turned with surprise and no little alarm to see what might be amiss.

They observed that one of the distant bullocks had begun moving, in what seemed an aimless and desultory manner, for it still cropped the grass as it walked, in the direction of Julia and Miss Yates. The latter, apparently panic-stricken at this approach, had run away hastily, and without taking sufficient care to look where she was going, in the opposite direction. The result being, that she had run herself into the little bog that surrounded the spring, and was now up above her ankles in soft, oozy mud, from which she was finding it almost impossible to extricate herself.

"Help! Help!" she called. "Help me—*quickly!*"

For the sight of the clamouring, gesticulating lady had aroused the curiosity of all the grazing cattle, and they began to move in the direction of Miss Yates, while the latter continued to scream and to struggle.

Julia stood still, making no attempt to go to the aid of her sister-in-law, and looking very impatient, as if she found the whole affair almost expressly designed to add to the provocations of the day.

"They will do you no harm, Charlotte, if you will only keep quiet and not shriek so!" she called irritably.

Susan eagerly summoned Mr. Wadham, whom she could see not far away among the trees, and he returned at a run, followed by William, who soon drove back the wandering cattle. The two men, with Susan, went to Miss Yates's assistance, and, by stepping gingerly on tussocks of reeds, were able to approach her, take her hands, and pull her out of the mire. One of her nankeen half-boots came off, but was rescued by Susan. All of the party became somewhat muddy during the rescue.

Limping and lamenting, Miss Yates was escorted into the grove, where she was sat down upon a fallen trunk, and restoratives administered by Mrs. Maddox, who carried smelling salts, and Miss Stanley, who had a flask of cologne in her ridicule. Miss Maria, the younger Stanley sister, shyly proffered a comfit, but this was coldly declined.

"What she needs is her lunch," said Mrs. Maddox.

The rest of the men now appeared on foot, severally, having tethered their horses on the far side of the grove. Tom eyed Miss Yates with ill-concealed impatience, and inquired,

"What is to do?"

He might well ask. The two little boys, having equipped themselves with sticks, were striking each other lustily and yelling at the top of their lungs, whether from pain or animosity it would be hard to judge.

"Should we not have the collation now?" suggested Susan. "I am sure a little food and drink will do everybody good."

"Collation? With all my heart," said Tom. "But here is no food to be seen. Baddeley does not appear to have arrived yet."

"How very singular! I told him that the cart, with the lunch, was to be here well before noon, and it is now after one o'clock."

"But *this* is not Stanby Wood," objected Julia.

"Stanby Wood? Who said that it was? Of course it is not Stanby Wood!" cried Tom. "Stanby Wood is three miles away across country."

"Well, that was where Baddeley was to take the collation, and so *I* told him, only last evening."

"My dear Julia—" exclaimed her brother, visibly reining in his feelings with a violent effort of restraint, "may I ask why in the world you did that?"

"Because I had understood—from *you*—that that was where we were to assemble—"

"I never said any such thing; or anything approaching it—"

While brother and sister thus accused one another, the rest of the party's thoughts dwelt sadly on the distant luncheon. Susan, in particular, recalling the care with which she and Mrs. Whittemore had planned the repast, began to feel that a malevolent star must be presiding over the excursion, and that the best thing they could all do was to go home.

The little boys set up a noisy and lugubrious clamour, on hearing that they were not to have anything to eat, and their mother made no attempt to hush them.

At this moment William suddenly gave the thoughts of the party a different turn by exclaiming,

"I had meant to make this announcement when we were all sitting down comfortably to luncheon, and cracking a bottle of wine, but as the luncheon and the wine are not to be had, I have no patience to be waiting any longer. Friends, congratulate me! I am the happiest man in Northamptonshire—for aught I know, in all of England! I have Mrs. Maddox's permission to tell you that Miss Harley has done me the honour to say that she will be my wife!"

It was then noticed that he was standing by Miss Harley and holding her hand, and that she, flushed pink as a wild campion, was looking very pretty and exceedingly happy.

A chorus of exclamation and congratulation followed on William's speech. Six of those present were unfeignedly happy, and loudly expressed their interest, pleasure, and satisfaction; Julia uttered a cool minimum of insincerities; Miss Yates, still sitting and sniffing on her fallen tree, said nothing at all, but darted one needle-like glance at Tom from the corners of her small sharp eyes. Tom, Susan saw with pain, looked utterly confounded, as if his world had fallen about his ears. He did, however, summon up enough resolution and self-command to bestow the proper compliments upon Miss Harley and his cousin William, though with how little heart to do so, perhaps only Susan guessed.

It was now generally agreed that, since the gentlemen had pronounced the wood an unsuitable site for excavation, being too damp and rocky, the party had best return to their carriages, and such as chose might then proceed to Stanby Wood, five miles by road, where they could possibly hope to find Baddeley with the refreshments. Susan suspected that the Yates family, from their general aspect, might prefer to return home directly, without taking any further part in the historical research.

Mr. Wadham did his best to conceal his disappointment in the turn that matters had taken. Walking back with Susan up the lane, he confessed to her that, privately, he had always considered the land around the cross-roads to be a likelier site than the wood for archaeological investigation—"These roads almost certainly being Roman, you see, Miss Price, and such a highly probable spot for a way-station or villa. But I fear that, just at present, the party are in no mood for spending any more time here."

Susan felt great sympathy with his thwarted aspirations; it did seem hard that he, the originator of the whole plan, should find his wishes and intentions entirely set aside.

"That is always the difficulty," she said, "with a large party; people in a group tend to be so unmanageable. If only the land around the cross-roads were of a more interesting nature, some of the party might wish to spend a little time here—"

It could not be denied, however, that the four fields surrounding the cross-roads were of a most prosaic and uninteresting character, being all ploughed over and grown with crops of young barley and oats respectively. The crops came close up to the hedgerows, the banks of the lanes were too steep to be sat on, and most of the party, by then, felt a decided inclination to quit the spot and go in search of rest and refreshment.

As they reached their conveyances, moreover, Mr. Noakes, the tenant who farmed the land, came riding up on his cob, curious to discover what a lot of grand folks' carriages were doing stopped by Stanby Stone Cross.

When informed by Tom that they were considering an excavation for Roman antiquities among his oats and barley, he became so very surly and contumacious that Tom flew into a passion, and told him that he was lucky not to be given notice on the spot.

Susan could not help sympathising with the farmer, who saw the fruit of his labours in danger from what must seem to him idle curiosity; it was on the tip of her tongue to dispute with Tom, but remembering the severe disappointment he had just undergone, she forebore; meeting Mr. Wadham's eye, instead, she gave him an imploring glance, and he, by a judicious mixture of irrelevant argument, and concurrence with both parties, succeeded in calming them down, pointing out that after the harvest, when there was nothing on the fields but stubble, would be an equally good time to investigate.

The little boys had begun to climb the steep banks and roll down, cuffing and kicking each other in the process, when several heavy drops of rain, succeeded by a loud clap of thunder, alerted the party to the fact that, while their minds were preoccupied with other cares, the fine weather had deserted them: clouds were piling up, the sky had turned very black, and a small sharp wind stirred the dust in the lane.

With cries of dismay the ladies hastily climbed into their respective conveyances, Tom neglecting to say goodbye to his sister and her friend, while Mrs. Maddox took a very friendly farewell of Susan, promising herself the pleasure of calling at Mansfield within a day or two so as to extend their knowledge of one another.

"Since you are to be Louisa's sister, dear Miss Price, in so short a time!"

"They are to be married so soon, then?" asked Susan, who had hardly, as yet, assimilated the astonishing fact of William's successful courtship of the heiress.

"Yes indeed. As soon as Captain Price is assured of his ship. He thinks it is to be the *Medusa*—but you will know all about that, I am sure. Louisa wishes to accompany him when he sails; she says that, of all things, the life of a sailor's wife is what she has always aspired to. We are all so rejoiced for her, Miss Price; your brother is the sweetest creature, and we think she cannot be in better hands."

"I am very happy that you have such a good opinion of him," Susan said warmly, and parted from the Maddoxes with very friendly feelings. Louisa gave her an impulsive kiss and called out of the carriage window, "You must come to Gresham Hill, Miss Price, and see my kittens!" as it rolled away, William and the Maddox brothers accompanying it on horseback.

By now the rain was commencing to fall in good earnest, and there were no more suggestions of a rendezvous to partake of the collation in Stanby Wood—supposing the collation to be there. None of the parties wished to do anything but hurry home.

Tom had already departed at a gallop on Pharaoh, and Susan, looking after him in considerable anxiety, settled herself as best she might to listen and reply to the good-natured congratulations of the Stanley sisters all the way home.

Chapter 9

BACK AT MANSFIELD, SUSAN COULD NOT HELP BEING STRUCK BY the contrast between the placid, harmonious decorum she found there, as Mrs. Osborne untangled Lady Bertram's tatting while she gave a description of the giant turtles in the Galápagos Islands, and the passionate and disagreeable emotions recently experienced during the unfortunate picnic.

Rain still continued to fall heavily, and thunder pealed outside, but in the calm, lofty and spacious rooms of Mansfield it was scarcely regarded.

"Ah, there you are, Susan," murmured her aunt. "We had wondered if the weather would cause you to return; it has become quite inclement, has it not? I did advise against your going, I believe. It is a good thing you came home."

Susan provided a brief account of the excursion, including the announcement of William's engagement to Miss Harley. She thought it might ease the pain for Tom if the first exclamations were over before he came in. Mrs. Osborne received the news with lively interest, Lady Bertram with more tranquillity.

"Louisa Harley is a good girl, and she will have thirty thousand. William has been fortunate; quite fortunate. I am not sorry that he will be connected with this neighbourhood. At one time I quite thought that Tom might offer for Miss Harley. But it is just as well he does not marry yet awhile.—Will you ring for candles, Susan? It grows too dark to see the colour of my silk. Where is Tom, by the bye?"

"Tom has not yet returned?" inquired Susan, not a little concerned. For he had started at the same time as Mr. Wadham's carriage, and might have been expected to return home considerably sooner.

But apparently he had not been seen; the servant who brought the candles had no news of him.

Shortly afterwards, however, as Mrs. Osborne was taking her leave and about to step into her brother's carriage, sheltered through the rain by Baddeley with an umbrella, a messenger came riding from the village to announce that Master Tom had been thrown from his horse and was just now lying senseless at the White House.

The ladies exclaimed in consternation. What could have caused the accident? What had been done for the victim? Who was caring for Tom?

"Twas that ill-conditioned young colt of his, Miss Susan; he were riding along the village street at a fair old gallop when there come a great clap o' thunder, as caused the nag to shy, and he threw Master Tom on the cobbles. Right outside the White House, he was throwed, and the lady said for to carry him in there, for she was a-looking from the window and saw it all, and Muster Crawford he rid off directly to fetch Dr. Feltham; and the lady sent me up here to tell you."

Upon hearing these very alarming tidings, Mrs. Osborne kindly abandoned her intention of returning to the Parsonage; instead she and Mr. Wadham remained with Lady Bertram and made some endeavour to soothe her agitated imaginings and restrain her fears until more definite information should be forthcoming.—In the meantime, all was wretched anxiety.

Susan sat blaming herself bitterly, though she could hardly have said for what: for not making more endeavour to dissuade Tom from riding Pharaoh to the picnic (not that her advice carried any weight with him); for not foreseeing the probable result of William's impulsive announcement and suggesting that he postpone it (but how could she have done so?); for not being able to prevent Julia from meddling and upsetting the arrangements (as if anyone could ever prevent Julia from doing exactly what she chose). Despite her knowledge of William's happiness, Susan could not help feeling extremely miserable, and wished deeply, not for the first time nor the last, that her sister Fanny were not so far away: dear, gentle Fanny who could always relieve agitation, heal hurts, and set everybody to rights.

And poor Mary Crawford, what a thing to happen outside her door, when she herself was in no fit state for such a disturbance! How shockingly must it have affected her! Particularly since it was Tom Bertram, who had refused to meet her and was in some sense her acknowledged enemy, to whom the mishap had occurred, who was now forced into her household.

In deep suspense and anxiety the three ladies sat together while Mr. Wadham talked calmly and sensibly of riding accidents in his experience that had caused very minor, trifling injuries, of medical skill, of Tom's sturdy appearance, and other such comforting topics. But it was a miserable time. Nothing outside could raise their spirits;

beyond the windows, the prospect was of wildly tossing trees and shrubs, of blossoms scattered on the grass, broken boughs, and paths awash with rain-water.

At last, by slow degrees, the wind abated, the sky cleared; by sunset the heavy clouds had dispersed, the air became clear and fresh once more. At this propitious time arrived another messenger from the White House: Mr. Crawford himself, come to bring them tidings of Tom.

"I make no apology, ma'am, for thus intruding on you; I know you must be stretched on a rack of anxiety."

Lady Bertram did not, perhaps, appear quite as anxious as *that;* but still she raised her eyes and kept them fixed on Mr. Crawford's face while he continued,

"Feltham has been with Sir Thomas continuously, and he now pronounces that there is no occasion for acute alarm. He does find a slight concussion, which renders it inadvisable for the patient to be moved at present; and the left arm is broken, but a simple fracture, fortunately, and that has already been set. Feltham is a most capable surgeon; I assisted him, and I assure you, ma'am, that His Majesty's surgeons themselves could have done no better. Your son is in excellent hands."

"But he is not at home!" lamented Lady Bertram. "He is at the White House, and that is so inconvenient, you know. How shall we be able to ascertain how he goes on?"

"Not to speak of the great—the very great—inconvenience to your sister—" here put in Susan. Mr. Crawford turned to her quickly.

"Pray do not regard that! She sent a message, begging you not to distress yourself, Miss Price, as she knew you would. But she asked me to assure you that the household is well able to manage; that there is not the least inconvenience in consideration; to be nursing your cousin, she says, will be, if anything, a useful distraction from her own state of health. And I am certain that she speaks the truth; my sister was ever one to rise to an emergency; she enjoys action and excitement far more than a quiet existence."

Susan could hardly believe this. *Once,* it might, perhaps, have been so; but now she could not feel that Mary Crawford really preferred the agitation of having a hurt young man in her house to the peaceful measure of her daily life. Nonetheless, Susan honoured the kind thought that sent the message, saw there was nothing to be achieved by protestations, and merely inquired, therefore, what needed sending down from the great house besides Tom's night-wear and toilet articles. Could they supply extra bedding, medicines, linen, additional servants?

"But sure, if we sent the large carriage—Tom would be best in his own home," repeated Lady Bertram again and again.

Mr. Crawford employed all his real kindness and intelligence in persuading her that this must not be; at least for twenty-four hours the injured man must remain where he was. Susan could not help admiring Crawford for the mild, friendly firmness with which he was reiterating the same facts over and over, showing not the least loss of patience or temper. He did it with such sympathy and natural ease that she must, in the silence of her heart, applaud him. Even Mr. Wadham could not have displayed more neighbourly perception and sensitivity.—She began to like him very well.

While Susan went to give instructions to the housekeeper as to needments for Tom, Mr. Crawford remained with the others in the drawing-room, talking, commiserating, advising, and, it was plain, endeavouring to give Lady Bertram's thoughts a more cheerful direction. When she returned, Susan heard him explaining that he had just taken a lease of Stanwix Lodge, a substantial house standing in its own grounds at a short distance outside the village of Mansfield.

"I felt I could not leave this neighbourhood until I had seen my sister's health take a decided turn for the better; but one is so uncomfortable staying for ever at an inn; and the White House is not large enough to accommodate me and my servants."

"Stanwix Lodge; yes, a very tolerable house." Lady Bertram's thoughts were satisfactorily diverted. "Admiral Leigh used to live there, and my husband, Sir Thomas the elder you know, used to visit him, and *he* said it was a very tolerable house, only the chimneys smoked abominably when the wind sets in the east."

"Well, since it is not the season for fires, that need not concern *me*," said Mr. Crawford, rising to take his leave.

After ascertaining that Lady Bertram was now in a reasonable state to be left, Mr. Wadham and his sister also announced that they would take their departure.

Susan thanked them warmly, all three, for their kindness and solicitude.

"I so much regret this melancholy ending to your Roman project," she told Mr. Wadham. "It has been a day of unexampled misfortunes—positively star-crossed. But I must hope for your sake that the scheme may not be laid aside for too long. We often have fine, dry weather in September, after the harvest—perhaps then—"

"But *then*, Miss Price, we must hope that your brother and sister will be safely restored to us," Mr. Wadharn said, smiling at her very kindly.

"Oh, to be sure—" Susan was quite surprised at herself that she could, even for a moment, have overlooked this fact. But the day had been over-full of happenings. "Could you not remain here for a few weeks after Edmund and Fanny have returned—you need not be going overseas again quite so soon, surely—?"

"My brother is fatally addicted to his duty, Miss Price," wryly remarked Mrs. Osborne. "If he feels that he is able to go, it will be next to impossible to restrain him."

Mr. Crawford lingered another moment, after the other two had left, in order to say,

"Mary sends you all kinds of messages, Miss Price, to the effect that, though in the present crisis she is aware that you can hardly be spared from Lady Bertram's side, she longs for a sight of you, however brief, should there be any moment when you can dare to slip away. I must warmly second her wish. I know—I have already discovered—the inexpressible pleasure and benefit that your visits afford her."

"Oh—" exclaimed Susan, blushing. "It is nothing—that is—we have so quickly become such friends."

Then, because she feared that he was about to ask her another probing question as to his sister's true state of health, and, just at that moment, she felt she had not the fortitude to answer him with the necessary composure, she continued, "I can imagine exactly what she wishes to hear. She is anxious for an account of today's excursion. And you may whet her appetite for horrors by telling her that every conceivable disaster befell us—a lady sank in the quagmire and was chased by wild bulls, my cousin nearly came to fisticuffs with a farmer who did not want his barley dug up, and the luncheon went astray and, so far as I know, has not yet been recovered. My cousin Tom's accident was but the fitting climax to such a day."

Mr. Crawford burst out laughing, but quickly hushed himself, recalling that he was in a house of mourning and anxiety.

"I will tell Mary," he said. "It will render her more than ever anxious to see you without delay," and he saluted Susan and went away.

On the following day Tom was found to be feverish, and although the broken bone was mending and the concussion had subsided, Dr. Feltham thought it inadvisable that he be moved for another two days, despite all Lady Bertram's exclamations and entreaties.

During the ensuing forty-eight hours, therefore, messengers plied back and forth very frequently between Mansfield Park and the White House. Mr. Crawford rode up almost every hour with news of the patient, and Mr. Wadham was hardly less assiduous.

On the second day, Mrs. Osborne kindly came to sit with Lady Bertram, and Susan herself was able to walk across the park and see how the patient did. She must feel that, although there was no question but that he would be receiving the kindest possible treatment, yet he could not help but be miserable and wanting a confidante; having sustained such an inconvenient and ignominious accident immediately after the news of Miss Harley's defection to another suitor, how could he be other than in the lowest and most wretched spirits?

She was received with the usual friendship and eagerness by Mary Crawford, who was up, and sitting in the front parlour, although so pale and haggard that Susan felt she had better be in bed.

"I know that you must be wearying to see how your cousin goes on, so I will not delay you for an instant," that lady said. "In spite of the fact that I am eaten to death with curiosity to hear the story of the ill-starred picnic from your side of the matter! Perhaps you will be able to spare me a few minutes after you have satisfied yourself as to the patient's well-being?—We have been obliged to put him in the back parlour, firstly because we are rather deficient in number of bedrooms, and secondly due to the fact that Feltham forbade us to carry him upstairs."

Susan, knowing how much Mary preferred sitting in her back parlour, which was the quieter, and took the sun, and had a door opening on to the garden, was impressed by the self-sacrifice which this represented.—She stept into the room and saw Tom lying upon a bed which had been arranged for him there, interestingly pale, propped against a pile of pillows, with his arm in a sling. Unshaved and with tousled hair, he looked a great deal younger than when he was up and dressed.

"Oh, Tom!"

"Hollo! Are you there, Susan? Is not this a plaguy business?" said he, endeavouring to speak with his usual lightness, but not altogether succeeding. "How do they all go on up at the house? Is Mama in a fine fret about me?"

"Of course she is! That is why I am come to see you! Every half-hour she is asking when Dr. Feltham will allow you home."

"Well, that is the devilish annoying part, Susan; he finds some trifling inflammation in my arm; I am sure it is no great matter, but these sawbones must always know best; he cannot allow me to be moved for several days yet. It is all cursed nonsense, you know; I am as fit as can be, and might be moved without the least trouble in the world; I hate to be giving all this inconvenience to Miss Crawford. She tells me, very good-naturedly, that she does not regard it, but, hang it all! this is her parlour, and she must want to be sitting here every minute of the day. There is the harp her brother brought her, and she has not had a chance of playing upon it. I feel very badly about the inconvenience that I am causing her, I do indeed; I wish you will say all that is proper to her about it, Susan."

Susan was interested. This, she thought, was the very first speech that she had ever heard Tom make, of such length, in which he truly entered into the needs and concerns of another person, and appeared to put their convenience before his own. The fact that the person in question was Mary Crawford, whom hitherto he had regarded as Mischief in being, was another sign of some radical change, which appeared to have overtaken him as a result of his accident.

Susan sat herself in a chair by the bed, observing that Tom did, in fact, look very pulled-down; his skin had a waxen tinge and there were black shadows under his eyes which made her willing to accept the doctor's verdict that he must not yet be moved.

"What of my horse, Susan? What of Pharaoh?" he asked directly. "Crawford was not able to tell me, but I made sure you would know. Was he hurt?"

"No, he has a swelled fetlock but is otherwise uninjured," she replied, having guessed that this was the first thing he would wish to know, and taken pains to make herself aware of the particulars. "Weatherby found him running loose in the park and brought him home."

"Thank goodness for that," said he, satisfied. "I would not have had Pharaoh injured for a thousand pound. When he is properly schooled he will make a famous clever animal in the field. But you were right, Susan; I should not have taken him out on Thursday; he was not ready for road work yet. That storm, though, was a wretched piece of ill fortune! I have been lying here thinking about it; if it were not for that last clap of thunder, all would have been well."

"And doubtless you were a little fatigued at that time," suggested Susan. "Your mind may have been less on the management of your horse, and more on the various evils and misadventures of the excursion."

She was wishing to lead up, by degrees, to Miss Harley's engagement; she thought it might be better for Tom to be speaking of it, not to let the wound bleed inwardly, and rankle, and poison him.

"Misadventures? Oh, ay, the collation went astray; that was thanks to Julia's cursed interference, I take it?"

"Yes, she had instructed Baddeley to send the cart to Stanby Wood."

"Perhaps that will teach her not to continually be meddling with matters at Mansfield. Let her govern her own household, and leave ours in peace. Julia is sometimes the outside of enough."

Whole-heartedly though Susan agreed with this statement, she was not going to be disparaging Tom's sister to him; she said,

"My brother William sent you his best and kindest regards. He was obliged to post up to London, you know, to the Admiralty; he was indeed sorry to be obliged to leave while you were laid up like this, and without bidding you goodbye."

"Ay, he is an excellent chap; I am sorry, too, not to see the last of him. I hope he may come this way again. I wish him all the good in the world. He is certain to become an admiral, you know; I think very well of William."

"He sent a message also," said Susan hesitatingly, "that he hoped very much it was not due to any action of *his*—the news, you know, the declaration that he had just made, concerning Miss Harley and himself—he was somewhat distressed by the notion that your accident might have been caused by absence of mind, by your concern over that announcement—"

Tom looked puzzled for a moment, thinking this out; then his brow cleared, and he gave a shout of laughter. "Oh, *now* I follow you, cousin! William thought I might be eating my heart out over his being handfast to Louisa Harley! It is no such thing! You believed me to feel ill-used because William had stept in and beat me to the post. No, no, I do not make any fling at him at all. It was entirely my own fault for not making a push to secure her favours earlier; but, now that it has happened, I do not in the least regret it. Louisa is a very good sort of girl, and will make William an excellent wife. In fact they are well suited. He is a capital fellow and thoroughly deserves her. But for *my* part (thinking it over) I am not sorry. She is sweet-tempered, to be sure; but her thoughts do not go deep."

Susan agreed gravely that this was so. Her heart felt immensely lightened.

Tom went on, "William's engagement has been making me think that when *I* marry, I would wish to secure a woman who has more of real intelligence than Louisa Harley; somebody that one can be talking to, whose advice one can be asking without getting some frittering reply; a woman of good sound judgment like Mrs. Osborne— or Miss Crawford. That is a woman in a thousand, you know, Susan!"

"She is indeed."

"I am very sorry, now, that I ever disparaged her," Tom continued, sinking his voice. "She has been so good, so kind to me. Susan, she is an angel! Here I come, disrupting her household to *such* a degree—and had not even had the civility to pay her a call previously—and she had been so ill, too. But she has not breathed a word of reproach, not a murmur; she has been so kind, so unaffectedly, spontaneously kind. And not in a martyred, forgiving way, you know, that one can't be tolerating; no, she can be very entertaining, wonderfully so! I do not wonder now that you have made such a friend of her. I have been wholly mistaken about her all this while, and I am very ready to admit it."

Susan gazed at him in silence, almost overwhelmed by the completeness of his recantation.

"And Crawford—you know—is a very decent sort of man. I find it hard, I must say, to believe those tales about him and my sister Maria."

Here Susan thought it her duty, since Tom was in such a conciliated mood, to disburden him of his errors of judgment due to the misinformation put about by Maria on this head; and to apprise him of the true story as she had it from Mrs. Osborne.—She did so, briefly and succinctly. Tom listened in silence, then said,

"That is just like Maria, you know. She was always spiteful, as a girl; I have known her, before, to tell tales of people that were not true, just to get her own back on them. I am very glad Crawford's name is cleared. I have always had an inclination to like him."

At this, Susan could not help blaming herself very heartily that she had not undeceived Tom sooner; but a more rational reflection soon showed her that in his previous state of mind it was highly improbable that he would have believed her.

He now reverted to Miss Crawford, and Susan had to listen to another paean of praise. She was so quick, so witty, so perceptive, had such depths, such strength of character, such understanding; she was so rare a creature, and beautiful, too; like a madonna, said Tom.

Giving patient ear to all this, Susan began to feel in herself a constriction of the heart. He loves her! was her thought. It is like Mr. Wadham all over again. After but two days in her company, he has come under her spell.

The conclusion could not be dismissed, and was easy to understand, since with so many of the eulogies that Tom was pouring out, Susan found herself in whole-hearted agreement. The conclusion was easy to understand, but not so easy to accept. She found that it gave her considerable pain. In Mr. Wadham's case she had been able to employ detachment. Here, that was not so.

Endeavouring to compose her spirits, she listened as Tom went on.

"My brother Edmund was used to be in love with her, you know, before he married Fanny. At the time I wondered at it; I thought her lively, pleasant enough, but nothing out of the common. In looks, you know, she was not to be compared with my sisters Maria and Julia; or so I then thought. I did not then understand her rare quality. She is like one of those heroines out of Shakespeare, you know," said Tom. "Portia, or Viola, one of those learned witty ones who can talk so well. *Now*, I wonder that Edmund did not make more of a push to secure her.—But of course there was all that cursed business about Maria and Crawford. It was a thousand pities. Still, Edmund married Fanny and did very well. And he would be too sober a fellow for Mary Crawford; she deserves a man with more spirit in him."

"Tom," said Susan gently—she felt her heart was almost breaking inside her as she spoke—"you are aware, are you not, that Miss Crawford is very, very gravely ill?"

Tom turned his eyes to hers. His hand lay on the coverlid; Susan took it and held it a moment.—She had never done such a thing before. Tom did not spurn her clasp; indeed he rather clung to her hand, as if he were beseeching her to make him some promise.

"She *looks* well enough," said he gruffly. "She needs—she needs only rest, and to be taken out of herself, I daresay."

"The doctor says—"

"Oh, the doctor! A doctor may not always perfectly understand such a case. Here has the doctor been shaking his head over my mother these twenty years, and I dare swear she will outlast us all."

Susan did not say that Lady Bertram was an indolent, selfish, self-indulgent woman, always prepared to fancy herself ill in order to avoid exertion, when there was nothing the matter with her save a lack of mental resources.

"All I meant, Tom, was that you should remember her frail state of health, and not be persuading her to attempt more than she ought, not be tiring or over-straining her."

"Of course I would do no such thing! I hope I am not such a boor as that."

Shortly afterwards, Susan took her leave. She sat with Mary Crawford in the front parlour for a short time, and gave her a somewhat curtailed account of the picnic, to which her friend listened with sparkling eyes.

"And so your brother William has won the heiress! Charming. It is no more than he deserves. I am very happy for him, and they will have a well-stocked *ménagerie* on board his ship, of parrots, guinea-pigs, and Barbary apes. And Miss Yates sank in the bog; that is just what one would wish for her. I am sorry that you were deprived of your luncheon. But I confess that I cannot be sorry about your cousin's accident, since it has afforded me the opportunity of recommencing our acquaintance. He is greatly changed,

Susan! I had remembered a rather thoughtless young man, wholly taken up with field sports and gambling, not a single serious nor an interesting idea in his head—but I find him much matured. He has more capacities, better parts than I had formerly believed. You were quite right in what you said to me about him; now I believe that he will, with time, turn into such a man as his father was. Mansfield will not lose by his stewardship.—I have a great idea of Mansfield, as you see, Susan," said Miss Crawford, laughing. "It is not the place—nor the trees nor stones—but the spirit of right behaviour, right ideas, of what we owe to our neighbours, and they to us. That is what Mansfield stands for, to me.—But I can see that you are on tenterhooks to return to your troublesome aunt. Loyal, self-denying Susan! It is too bad that you have to spend so much time in such service. Let us hope, however, that Fate is preserving a plum for you to pull out of the pudding. There! Give me a kiss and be on your way. I need not ask for you to come again soon; so long as your cousin is under this roof I am assured of your daily visits."

"You are assured of them *without* his presence," said Susan, a little stung, and had another kiss blown at her as she walked out of the door.

Outside she found Henry Crawford just dismounting from his curricle. He immediately offered to drive her back across the park, an offer she was glad to accept, since she found herself, perhaps from the unwonted exertions of the previous days, more than commonly tired.

Henry, with true gentlemanly perception, seeing her somewhat absent and preoccupied, did not fatigue her with over-much conversation, though he did take pains to reassure her as to Tom's condition; the inflammation, he said, would pass, he himself had suffered from just such a fever with a broken arm, but a few days had brought him complete recovery, and now he never thought of it; one arm was just as serviceable as the other, he could hardly recall which one had been broken. Tom would surely be back home in a few days, none the worse for his experience.—After which comfortable assertion, he allowed the conversation to die away into a friendly silence. They did not speak of Mary's health, except for Susan's once saying,

"I see you have brought your sister a harp. She must be very delighted with it. It is too bad that it stands in my cousin's sickroom, and at present she is debarred from practising upon it."

"Not wholly debarred," he replied. "I understand that she has promised to play to your cousin so soon as he is equal to the experience, and he has expressed himself eager to hear her. But she says that she is not able to play for very long at a time; she finds it tiring."

Susan did not comment on this; they understood one another too well. It was singular: she began to feel that she had been knowing Henry Crawford for years.

On the sweep she was disheartened, though hardly surprised, to see Julia's barouche. Mrs. Yates had, of course, been informed by note of Tom's accident, and was now come, all sisterly concern, to find out how he did. Charlotte had not accompanied her (a small mercy for which Susan was duly thankful); Miss Yates had found herself quite prostrated after her various misadventures at the picnic, and had been laid down for several days upon her bed.

Julia was sitting with Lady Bertram and Mrs. Osborne. They inquired eagerly how Tom did, and Susan was able to give them sufficient reassurance as to his condition; though his mother was greatly disappointed that he still was not permitted to come home.

"Sure they can do nothing for him at the White House that we could not do better here."

Susan, recalling the profound effect that Miss Crawford was having upon him, could not agree, but kept her opinions to herself.

"Stupid fellow!" cried Julia. "I have no sympathy with Tom! He brought all his misfortunes upon himself! And John says the same! Why should he ride to the picnic on that vicious, half-trained colt? It was vanity—pure, boastful, idiotic thoughtlessness! And he was abominably rude to Miss Yates— did not inquire after her hurts, hardly addressed a word to her throughout, never said goodbye: she was perfectly mortified by such usage. I have no patience with Tom. It is certainly most unfortunate that he should now be laid up in the house of those talking, scheming, encroaching Crawfords—but he has only himself to thank for his troubles, after all.—I suppose the Crawfords will now expect to be received in *this* house. Well *I*, for one, do not intend to resume the acquaintance. I understand from Mrs. Osborne, here, that the affair with my sister Maria was not quite as represented—or perhaps not—but, for my part, I think there is no smoke without fire. I believe there may be things to be said on both sides. I never liked Henry Crawford—a sly, self-confident, insinuating sort of man—and his sister was no better. She always had an eye to the main chance. I intend to cut the connection, and I strongly advise you, ma'am—" turning to her mother "to do the same."

"Oh dear," sighed Lady Bertram. "It is all very unfortunate. Very disagreeable. But I will wait and see what Tom says, when he returns home."

Susan could not help but smile, inwardly, as she imagined what Tom's comments would be, on his mother applying to him for such advice.

To give the conversation another turn, Mrs. Osborne here kindly inquired whether the travellers in the West Indies had lately been heard from.

"Oh, I daresay *they* will never come back to England," responded Julia carelessly. "Edmund manages my father's business so prosperously, I understand, that 'tis all Lombard Street to a China orange Tom will ask him and Fanny to remain in Antigua and continue to act as agents.—Indeed, why should they return? I hear the climate is delightful—the planters live like princes, a man may have twenty servants who in England would have but two; they will be very stupid if they do not settle out there and remain for the rest of their lives."

Susan was aghast at such a notion, which had never occurred to her. But she saw there might be considerable reason in what Julia had said. The family estates would always prosper far better if there were an intelligent, conscientious man on the spot to undertake their management; who better for the purpose than Edmund? And he might well consider it his duty to remain; his calling as a minister of the church could be followed as well in Antigua as in Northamptonshire. And if he remained, Fanny, naturally, would remain with him.

Susan was not at all sure that she was able to endure the prospect of such a severance. Fanny was her dearest friend, her favourite sister, her confidante and mentor in all anxieties and troubles. Just at present she was missing Fanny unspeakably, and her principle, her only comfort was the pouring out of her thoughts to Fanny in long letters. The idea that, for the rest of her life, communication with her sister must be reduced to such a cumbrous and slow process was not one that she could tolerate with equanimity.

—Fortunately she recalled that Julia had a tolerably strong dislike of Fanny; and, furthermore, generally found herself in total disagreement with her brother Edmund's feelings and ideas. What Julia wished, she tended to believe must be the case; therefore, because she hoped it, she felt certain that Fanny and Edmund would never return to Mansfield.

"By the bye, ma'am." continued Julia, "I have heard a piece of news that may well astonish you! My sister Maria, who is now, you know, married to Ravenshaw, has come into this country."

"Dear me! Is that so?"

"Lord Ravenshaw, it seems, is a close friend of the Duke of Brecon, and so the pair of them, Maria and her new husband, are staying with the Duke at Bellamy, where he has a large party assembled for the races. I must say, it is rather like Maria's impertinence, to force herself in where she is not wanted, so close to her former acquaintance."

"Presumably the Duke of Brecon wanted her," observed Susan.

Julia lifted her brows in a haughty stare.

"I beg your pardon, cousin? Perhaps you were not aware that the Duke of Brecon is the most profligate old wretch, with, I daresay, half a dozen mistresses and nothing good to be said of him, save that he is as rich as Dives."

"How very scandalous," sighed Lady Bertram.

"I trust that you will not be receiving my sister Maria, ma'am?"

"How can I tell? I do not know what to think," said Lady Bertram. "I shall ask Tom."

"It will be very disgraceful if they appear with the Duke's party at the Northampton Assemblies. My own sister! I shall hardly know where to look."

"Perhaps it might be advisable for you to refrain from going to the Assemblies while you know that my cousin Maria is in the country," suggested Susan.

"What? Be kept away from such entertainments as the district has to offer, because of my sister Maria? A likely thing, indeed! I will thank you to be keeping your advice to yourself, Cousin Susan, if that is the best you can offer."

Somewhat ruffled, Julia took her leave. She was displeased that Lady Bertram had made no definite commitment of refusing to see Maria; and annoyed that Mrs. Osborne had remained in the room throughout her visit, for she had intended to impress on her mother, now that Louisa Harley was out of the way, the necessity for instructing Tom that he must now bestir himself and offer for Miss Yates.

THE RECOVERY OF TOM BERTRAM, AS HENRY CRAWFORD HAD
prophesied, was but a matter of days; the inflammation died
down, his appetite came back; he was able to sit up in bed, then to
walk; then Dr. Feltham pronounced that he might be taken home
in the carriage.

He could not leave the White House without regret, although
fully aware that it was only proper in him to do so as soon as possible.

"But to be there, listening to her conversation, listening to her
angelic performance upon the harp," he said. "Oh, Susan! It has
entirely changed my life. I do believe that it has changed my life."

Susan quite believed him. She could see the change. Susan was
Tom's confidante at this time—and the weight of his confidence was
both pleasure to her and pain. He was not yet strong enough to be out
of doors for more than an hour or so, nor to be occupied within doors
very continuously; in consequence of which there was a great deal of
time left to walk about, and fret, and talk to his cousin, while Lady
Bertram nodded over her tapestry and Pug snored. Susan found these
confidential sessions very tiring; particularly as the questions put to her
by Tom, over and over, "Do you think my being in the White House

fatigued her? Did her harm? Or did she, could she, find any pleasure in my company?" were exceedingly difficult to answer.

One escape from Tom's questions was to walk down to the White House to see Mary for herself; and this at least was powerfully seconded by Tom, who, every morning and every evening would exhort her to do so.

"Do you not think you should visit Miss Crawford and find out how she goes on? Take the chaise, cousin, if you feel tired. I will sit with my mother."

Tom had never been so mild, so thoughtful, so considerate.

The reason why Susan found Tom's questions hard to answer was because she thought his visit *had* done Mary considerable harm; drained her of what small vitality she had left, depleted her dwindling resources. And yet, there was also no doubt that she had found enjoyment in his company; *that,* she herself freely admitted. And her questions were almost as difficult to answer as Tom's.

"Did I do wrong, my dearest Susan, in practising my art upon him, just a little? I found it such a pleasure! Even more so than practising upon the harp—and much less fatiguing! I could hardly avoid being a trifle proud that I had not lost my former skill through lack of exercising it.—I do assure you that, with Tom, I was not behaving like a coquette; never less so. At first, I cannot deny, there was a degree of satisfaction in triumphing over a mind so conditioned to dislike, so filled with prejudice against me. But my conduct has been thoroughly guarded at all times; he was never in the least danger of over-excitation, I promise you."

Susan was fascinated, almost frightened, almost repelled. She had never before heard Mary in this vein; it was like witnessing the final stages of a conflagration in some great mansion, when the flames, which the firemen had thought extinguished, suddenly leap out of an upper window with terrifying power to annihilate all within their reach.

"It has been of absorbing interest to me, Susan, to observe his altered manner. I recall him in the old days!—so careless, so self-satisfied, so confident that any woman would be delighted to accept him if he should be pleased to offer for her; as, indeed, he must lately have been in regard to Miss Harley. This has been a salutary month for Master Tom. And he has been wholly unaware of my objective—like true art, concealed and interwoven in its own medium. I won him over entirely by serious conversation. He has never, it is very plain, been in the company of a woman of intelligence before—excepting your own, my love, and since he has been used, from the first, to regard you as an inferior being, the likelihood of your true value has never even occurred to him. I return him to you at the very least a greatly improved companion, capable of rational conversation, his mind opened to receive the possibility of new ideas. I may hazard a guess that he is *half* in love with me, and since it is plain that he has never been anything like near to losing his heart before, that cannot but be doing him good. Love is a civilising influence on a young man."

Susan listened in silence, wondering at her friend's animation. This was a different Mary indeed! the difference between the cat asleep on the hearthstone and the same cat at full stretch in pursuit of a mouse. It was a Mary that she had never known before.

Mary observed her expression, paused, and smiled.—They were sitting in the garden, under the shade of a thick mulberry tree. An arrangement of three chairs, set together, with cushions and the canvas back-rest, had been made for Mary's comfort, yet it was evident that she was in pain. A muscle contracted in her cheek from time to time. The day was an exceedingly close one; after the storm that had caused Tom's accident, the fine weather had returned, even warmer than before; hot July was turning to sultry August.

"I hope I do not shock you, my dear Susan? I believe I could not speak so to our beloved Fanny; but you are of a robuster nature. And these things must, they ought to be thought of. The relations between men and women should not be a matter of chance; as our behaviour in all other aspects of life is governed by the acquired skill of intelligent good manners, so should the most important area of all, between the male and female sex. My art, like the potter's guiding hand, has transformed Tom into something more approaching a useful domestic vessel; some female unknown to me (not Miss Yates, I hope) will, in future, have cause to thank me, though by that time I shall be long forgotten."

Susan here made some inarticulate exclamation of distress, a jumbled sentence in which "cooler weather of autumn," "Fanny's return" and "change of medical treatment" were intertangled. But Mary smiled and shook her head.

"No, my dear, *I* am not deceived, and I shall take it as a kindness if *you* will now disabuse yourself of any such fanciful notions. Argument is a waste of our valuable time together. I shall not be seeing Fanny. My time is measured in weeks, if not in days. I have asked our kind Frank Wadham to bring me the Sacrament soon, while I am in my right mind, before I become too weak and wandering to follow the service.—You stare, to hear me talk so, directly after having expressed myself in such a very different vein. But I am as I was made. If, in my life, I have done harm through thoughtlessness, I trust that it was not so *very* bad, and that I am atoning for it now. For my part,

I think that a little flirtation is far less of a sin than vindictiveness, or arrogance, or pride; and of those I have not been guilty."

"No indeed!"

"I have sent for an attorney, dear Susan, in order to arrange my last bequests; for I should greatly dislike the Ormiston family to be benefiting in any way by my decease. They have sufficient gold of their own. What I leave—and it is not much; I have been a thriftless grasshopper, not a prudent ant—I leave to you, my love, so that you need not be applying to your cousin Tom when you are in need of a new gown; my legacy will not provide you with much more than that."

Susan exclaimed again, a wordless cry of protest, sorrow, and gratitude, which Mary brushed aside.

"Now listen: what I wish to say to you is of importance. Kindly pay close attention. I am laying no command on you—no behest, no exhortation. I do not care for deathbed dramatics, and I detest the notion of a dead hand reaching out from the past to govern people's actions. But it would fulfill a very dear hope of mine if you and Henry were to come together in marriage."

"Oh—but—"

"Hush! I do not ask—I do not question. Henry has a high—a very high opinion of you, I know. He has never seen another woman, after Fanny, whom he could *possibly* consider as a wife—excepting yourself. You are the first. And he would be a good husband—kind, considerate, loving, provident. You would be looked after, cared for, most devotedly; an experience which, I think, must be new to you," said Mary with a faint smile. "But it may not come to pass; I make no reservation, no demand; I have no right. One of the lessons I have learned, here at Mansfield, is that we must not seek to govern one another. I learned it from you, my love—among other things."

"From *me?*"

"Among other virtues, you have that of being blind to your own merit!—But here is Henry, come to drive you home; and indeed it is time. I have made myself quite breathless with preaching at you, poor Susan; and you have others beside me to care for. Pray, pray bring little Mary here tomorrow, to rummage in my writing-desk; and give my sincerely affectionate greetings to Tom."

Weak and breathless though she had rendered herself, the parting smile she gave Susan had something in it of her old wicked sparkle.

Susan's being driven home by Henry was now an established thing; very often they did not speak at all on the way, or only of simple matters, the weather, the harvest, what kind of fruit might be procured for Mary; but they were at ease together, the companionable ease of brother and sister. On this occasion, Susan did not feel that what Mary had just said to her in any way changed the tenor of their relationship.

Sometimes Henry came into the great house, to talk with Lady Bertram a little, or play a short game of billiards with Tom, who was now very nearly restored to normal health. If Julia's carriage were to be seen outside, Henry tactfully did not enter the house; he knew that Mrs. Yates regarded him with abhorrence and could hardly spare the pains for bare civility to him, should they chance to meet.

In mid August came a batch of letters from the West Indies; one from Fanny, for Susan, one from Edmund, for Tom. Edmund's letter told of business prosperously completed, and gave a date for their departure from Antigua, a date now long since passed, for the letter had been written in June and announced that they would embark in July.

"So already, at this time, they are on the sea!" exclaimed Susan joyfully.

The thought of her sister's return was inexpressibly relieving to her; she felt that she could hardly bear to wait with patience the necessary weeks remaining before the arrival date. All day she carried Fanny's letter about with her, like a talisman.

"I have written to Mary Crawford by the same mail," wrote Fanny; and at evening Susan walked down, over the hot, limp grass, with little Mary, to discover if this letter, also, had been received.

She found that it had. She found Mary in a remarkable state, visibly weaker, as she now grew day by day, yet flushed, touched, elevated, as if she had been witness to some miraculous event.

"No, I will *not* tell you what Fanny said to me! I see that you had a letter from her too. But such letters are private—not to be shared, not even by one's dearest friend. Fanny herself would not wish it. And I do not ask to hear what she has said to you. I can see that it has made you happy; that is the main thing.

"Come here, now, little Mary, and I will show you how the ancient Greeks used to make sacrifices to their gods; hand me tinder and taper from the writing-desk, and we shall have a fine bonfire."

While the child watched with wondering eyes, Mary carefully burned her letter, page by page, on the flagstones of the terrace.

"There! It is all gone into thin air. Now, little one, you must blow the ashes away—puff out your cheeks and blow—so! And when you are an old, old lady, you will remember blowing those pages away and wonder what was written upon them."

A week later Susan found Frank Wadham outside the White House when she paid her evening visit.

"I have administered the Sacrament," he said. "Feltham says, and I agree, that she is not likely to last the night. She came over very faint a while since; Elinor has made her some mint tea, but she could only take the smallest sip. Go in: she has been hoping to see you. She is in the back room; she was too weak to climb the stair, and did not wish to be carried."

Susan found Mary in the bed that had been provided for Tom. The door and window to the garden stood open, for it was another breathlessly hot evening, with not a hint of wind. Henry was in the garden, walking up and down on the terrace.

"Do you feel much pain, dear Mary?" Susan asked.

Mary slightly moved her head in negation. She had not strength to speak for the moment; but she raised her brows with a slight, wry smile at her friend, and, after a little while, murmured, "I think these must be the pangs of death. They are certainly like no other! Except, perhaps, those of birth: but my own birth—I do not remember; and of any other—I have no experience . . ."

Her voice died away. Elinor Osborne came into the room with a napkin dipped in lavender water, which she proffered, but Mary wordlessly waved it away. Her head moved a little, continuously, on the pillow, but she said no more, except once, faintly, "I wish it would rain!"

Henry came in and stood by the empty hearth. Susan stept to the door, but he caught at her hand, as if imploring her to remain; and indeed she had no thought of returning to the great house, she had meant merely to retire to the front room. Tom had promised to remain with his mother should his cousin find herself unable to leave Mary. "Give her my love," he had muttered hoarsely, and Susan had faithfully passed on the message, which was received with the same faint, wry smile.

At midnight a heavy pattering commenced on the leaves of the mulberry tree outside; it could plainly be heard, for the casement still stood wide open.

"Hark!" said Susan. "It rains!"

Mary's dark eyes moved towards the window; she gave a small sigh of pleasure. The patter outside increased to a drumming; through the window came a scent of wet grass and vegetation. No sound but the rain could now be heard.

"It is a fine rain!" whispered Mary. "A fine, drenching rain."

She sighed again, moved a little as if seeking a more comfortable position, and was still.

"She has gone," said Elinor quietly.

Henry moved to the bedside and closed her eyes.

They sat on beside her, all reluctant to leave the room, listening to the solemn, continuous drumming of the rain on the terrace and on the grass.

"So," remarked Mrs. Yates, walking into Lady Bertram's drawing-room, "so, Mary Crawford has died at last. Well, she will be no loss. Mansfield will be the better for the lack of her presence at the White House. She should never have come here; it was a most impertinent intrusion. I suppose, now, that the brother will go away again, and that also will be an excellent thing."

Susan, who had been sitting at the far end of the room, unseen by her cousin, sorting out a basket of wools, here quietly rose to her feet and walked towards the door.

"I should be obliged, ma'am," she said, pausing there to address Julia, "if you would not be speaking so of Miss Crawford in my presence. I consider that her character exemplified all that was excellent, in virtue, sense, and taste; she was my great friend. I will not remain to hear ill things spoken against her."

"Hey-day!" cried Julia, very much ruffled, as Susan left the room. "Here's a great to-do about a trifle. I should like to know what right *she* thinks she has to prevent my speaking my mind in my own home."

"But this is not your home, you know," said Lady Bertram. "Your home is at Shawcross."

Ignoring her mother's mild remark, Julia continued, "It was not before time that pernicious woman died, if she was to be putting such ideas into my cousin's head. And I daresay you will be glad enough, ma'am, not to have Susan continually running off down to the White House, as she has been wont to do during these last months."

Tom walked into the room, looking spent and haggard. He said to his mother, "I thought it right, ma'am, to call at the White House and leave your respects and condolences as well as my own. Mr. Crawford asks to be remembered to you and thanks you."

"Did you see the corpse?" inquired Julia. "How does it appear? When is the funeral to be? Does Mr. Wadham conduct the service?"

"It is to be at the Church of the Holy Sepulchre in Northampton," said Tom. "Mr. Wadham will assist at the service but it will be conducted by the Bishop of Oxford who, it seems, is a friend of Mr. Crawford."

"Oh—! How singular! In that case, however, I suppose there is no necessity for us to go. If it had been here in the village it might have been otherwise. I certainly shall not go, and I am sure you need not, ma'am."

"I intend to go," said Tom quietly. "The funeral will take place on Tuesday. If you wish to attend it, ma'am, I shall be very glad to escort you."

"Oh dear," said Lady Bertram. "No; I do not think I shall go. Funerals are so very fatiguing. And then, the drive to Northampton is so disagreeable. Besides, I have not seen Mary Crawford in so many years; not since that other time when she and her brother were staying at the Parsonage. No, I shall not undertake such a journey. If you attend, Tom, that will be sufficient."

Julia eyed her brother sharply and asked, "Is your fever come back, Tom? You do not look at all the thing."

"No, I am well. It is nothing.—I have asked Crawford to dinner here, ma'am, this evening; it is not right that he should be alone at such a time."

"Do you think that really necessary, my love? Cannot he go to the Parsonage?"

"Wadham and his sister have been with Crawford continually as it is."

"Very well. If you think it right. I daresay you will remind Susan to tell Baddeley."

Julia, who had looked very far from approving at this announcement, now remarked,

"It is certainly highly inconvenient that all this should be taking place *here*. I suppose, in order to satisfy the dictates of civility, you must have Crawford here, but it is not at all what one would be wishing.—*Such* a connection!—Speaking of which, Tom, I think you had best, at this juncture, drop a hint to our cousin—or perhaps *you* would be the properest person to do it, ma'am—not to be quite so close and confidential with the gentleman as, I am informed, has lately been the case. Day after day to be driving here from the village in his curricle: it is not at all the thing; very far, Lady Bertram, from the way in which you brought your own daughters up to behave."

"Susan has a great deal of sense and propriety," said Lady Bertram placidly. "I am not at all afraid of her behaving herself unladylike."

"Just the same, I think she had better look out for herself. I think, Tom, you had better ask the gentleman his intentions. Yes, *that* would be best. Although he is certainly very far from the kind of match that one would wish for one's *friends,* for Susan, Crawford will do well enough; indeed, she will be exceedingly lucky to fix him. Six thousand a year and the place at Everingham; it is far above what she has any claim to be expecting. A little trouble on your part, Tom, will bring it off and secure for her a satisfactory settlement. Yes, you must have a talk with him, and the sooner the better, while the demise of his sister leaves him in a softened, undecided mood, ready to be pleased with any female who will have him. And such a girl as Susan is certainly all that *he* has a right to expect."

By the end of this speech Mrs. Yates had worked herself to such a pitch of enthusiastic planning that she quite smiled on her mother and brother.

Lady Bertram had not been able to follow her argument very closely; she said in a perplexed tone,

"Does Mr. Crawford offer for Susan? I thought that it was *Fanny* that he had a partiality for; but that, you know, came to nothing, for she married dear Edmund."

Tom said irritably, "Julia seems to think, ma'am, that he has been paying Susan attentions; I have seen nothing but what was proper, myself."

"Well, if that is the case, Tom, you had best ask the gentleman what he intends, and so secure him."

"But you would not wish to lose Susan, ma'am?"

"If a gentleman of good estate offers for her, I should raise no objection. It would be her duty to have him, indeed; it is every young woman's duty to accept such an offer."

Both ladies now became greatly engaged in the plan of marrying Susan off to Mr. Crawford, Lady Bertram from disinterested, Julia from highly interested motives. If Susan were once out of Mansfield, sheer inconvenience would soon, Julia shrewdly perceived, drive Tom into matrimony.—While Lady Bertram merely felt that if a man of substantial means such as Mr. Crawford remained unmarried, it was almost a matter of morality that some young woman should attach him; and Susan was a very good girl; if he were available, then she should have him.

This decided, both ladies went to work on Tom at such length and with so lively a persistence that at last, miserable, guilty, dejected, and goaded beyond endurance, he made a kind of promise to do as they recommended, and so escaped them.

His opportunity did not come for several days, not until after the funeral, which was attended by both Tom and Susan. Mrs. Osborne also sat in their pew; Mr. Wadham read the lessons, and the sermon, a very affecting one on the text "They shall not grow old," was preached by the Bishop.

Henry Crawford sat by himself and they respected his wish for privacy; Susan, as always, had the greatest reluctance to push herself forward, and she had said everything that was possible to him during several earlier meetings; she had been seeing him repeatedly since his sister's death, because, as Mrs. Osborne had said, and Susan agreed, he was so very severely afflicted that without continual company he would hardly hold up.

After the service they were obliged to hasten away. Julia had agreed to sit with Lady Bertram, but said she could not remain upwards of two hours; little Tommy had thrown out a rash and she feared that it might be the chicken-pox.

The tiny group of mourners in the churchyard soon dispersed and went their several ways. Susan, glancing back as they drove off, at the grave mounded with its wreaths of late roses, could see only one lady remaining, who appeared to be studying the wreaths and their inscriptions; the lady, richly dressed in velvet with a feathered hat, bore no evidence of mourning and was not familiar to Susan, who thought that perhaps she was merely a passer-by, not connected with the obsequies at all. On the drive home the strange lady was soon forgotten, since poor Tom was unburdening himself, as he did at least once a day, on the subject of his guilt and wretchedness.

"I hastened her end, Susan. Without question, I hastened her end; if it were not for my blundering stupidity, if I had not taken advantage of her kindness, battened on her, worn out the remains of her strength and resources—I believe she would be with us still."

"It could have been only a matter of time, Tom," Susan repeated gently, as she had on many similar occasions. "Everybody knew that; Dr. Feltham knew it; indeed he confessed himself astonished that she had lasted so long. It was the air of Mansfield, he said; anywhere else, in such a case, she must have succumbed far sooner. Her constitution was quite worn out."

"But if I had not invaded her tranquility—cut up her peace—she might have remained alive long enough to see Fanny—and that was her chiefest wish. I can never forgive myself for that—never!"

"You must forgive yourself, Tom, for *she* had done so; indeed she told me repeatedly that she was glad of the opportunity for getting to know you better; which otherwise, you know, she would never have done."

"No, because I was such a bigoted, churlish dolt that I would not go to call upon her! Oh, Susan, I am very miserable, indeed! All my behaviour has been at fault. Oh, how deeply I wish she were still with us."

He could not wish it more deeply than Susan did herself. Every minute she found herself longing for the playful, light-hearted common sense of her friend, who would have been teasing Tom for the self-importance of his grief, and scolding him out of excessive guilt. The burden of his continual self-reproaches was a hard one for Susan to endure, combined, as it was, with the frequent need to be comforting Henry Crawford in his more intense, more rational, less vocal affliction.

She had been walking half an hour with Henry in the shrubbery at Mansfield one evening later that week when, seeing Tom approach, she made her excuses and slipped away along a side-path. She did not feel equal to the combined wretchedness of the pair of them, and hoped that, left together, they might find a means to comfort each other.

—She had been asking Henry his plans, and he had told her that he had none.

"This has been such a bitter blow, Miss Price. I know that you warned me; I see now that you did your best to warn me again and again; but somehow I could not bring myself to believe the truth. I think that it will take me a very considerable time to accept it, even now, even after the event. I believe that I shall travel; to be continually on the move is the only prospect that I can tolerate. Tomorrow I leave Mansfield, first for Norfolk, then I know not where. Perhaps I may go to China."

Susan found herself envying his freedom, though not his state of mind, as, leaving the two men, she rambled off along a narrow glade. Oh! she thought, the pleasure of such infrequent moments of solitude! The relief of being thus private with one's own thoughts, of having no demands made upon one for sympathy, entertainment, assistance, understanding, support.

Hardly had she framed the thought when, to her astonishment, she heard her own name spoken.

The two men were still not far away from her, though screened, in the little wilderness with its winding walks, by no more than a thicket of syringa; she could clearly hear the voice of her cousin Tom, now demanding in extremely forthright terms whether Mr. Crawford intended to marry his cousin Miss Price, and, if not, whether he had considered how severely he was compromising her by being thus continually and so confidentially in her company?

It was the voice of the old Tom, the old hectoring, domineering Tom, whom Susan had thought banished for good in the reformation wrought by Miss Crawford.

She stood aghast, thunderstruck. For a moment she felt almost stunned with outrage. To hear her name bandied thus—as though *she* were to have no say, no choice in the matter—she, who had been expending herself, hour after hour, day after day, in the consolation of those very two who now appeared to be discussing her as if she were some insentient being without a will of her own!

Picking up her skirts she ran swiftly back through the windings of the maze until she confronted the two of them once more.

Her eyes flashing with indignation—*"Stop!"* she exclaimed. "I will not have this! It is unjust, it is undignified! Pray, Tom, be silent this instant, and never let me hear you touch on this topic again. I am *not* a—a marketable commodity to be offered for barter like some piece of furniture. As for you, sir—" to Mr. Crawford—"I can only apologise deeply that you have been subjected to such embarrassment. Pray endeavour to overlook it. I—I am very unhappy that our last meeting should have been attended with such mortification. —I will now bid you goodbye."

Unable any longer to withhold her tears she hastily turned away and almost ran from them, leaving them no less aghast than she herself had been.

Chapter 11

FOR SOME DAYS, TOM AND SUSAN HARDLY SPOKE TO ONE ANOTHER. The good understanding that had been building between them seemed destroyed for ever; she could not forgive him for his officious, insensitive interference, while he was as much astonished and wounded by her behaviour as if the stock he were tying around his neck had turned into an adder and bit him.

Mr. Crawford left Mansfield on the day following the scene in the shrubbery. But before doing so he wrote a letter to Susan:

My dear Miss Price:

Like you, I very deeply regret that our last meeting should have been clouded by the unfortunate and unnecessary encounter with your cousin. I do not blame him; he was but doing his duty; I do blame myself for my inconsiderate behaviour, for not thinking less of my own needs and more of your good name. Your recent kindness has been of such inestimable benefit to me; I can truly say that I do not think I would have survived after the recent tragic event without the support of your friendship and solicitude. I value it inexpressibly. And—if your cousin had not intervened at that moment—I think it not improbable that I would have implored you to add to your previous generosities by becoming my companion for life—such is the dependence I have fallen into the habit of placing upon you.

I do not ask this now. You, rightly enraged by your cousin's interference, would, might, feel that I was forced to do so by his exigency. The position would be falsified. Our relations would be forced, fettered by the unfortunate circumstances of their commencement.

And yet I find myself still hoping, feeling, that, in the future, when sorrow has died down and humiliation is forgotten, it may not be impossible for us to meet again, for me to put the question that I do not put now, for you to consider the possibility of our union. As to myself, I would welcome it eagerly. I have the deepest admiration for your person, your intelligence, your goodness, your sagacity. You would make me, I am sure, a very happy man. And, if devotion, care, consideration, could achieve it, I believe I could make *you* happy. And I know that, from beyond the grave, Mary would smile, to see what she had been hoping for come about.

Your sincere friend,
Henry Crawford.

After she had read this letter, cried over it, and read it again, Susan resolutely put it away. I will not think about it, she said to herself. Not for a long time. I will wait, and show it to Fanny; until I see her again, I will think no more of it.

Naturally, this was a very hard resolution to keep. Naturally she *did* think of the letter, a great deal; but she adhered to her resolve not to reread it. Such strength of mind was reinforced by a new spiteful tale from Julia, who came into Lady Bertram's room a few days later, exclaiming,

"Well, here is a fine thing! Here has Crawford been seeing Maria again, under our very noses!"

"Indeed?" feebly from Lady Bertram. "How very shocking!"

And from Tom, much more sceptically, "How do you know such a thing as *that,* Julia? Who is your informant?"

"Why, Charlotte Yates's sister, Lady Digweed, was in Northampton lately, buying boots for her children, and she saw the pair of them! Conversing, would you believe it, like old friends! Can you imagine anything so disgraceful?"

"Why should it be disgraceful for Mr. Crawford to converse with a lady whom he has once known?" here quietly inquired Susan. "Unless you feel that, because Maria left her first husband, anybody must be disgraced who talks with her?"

Ignoring this, Julia continued. "It was the day of the funeral. There they were, in the churchyard. He was standing by the grave, and she came up and spoke with him. Lady Digweed saw them both, as near as I am to you. By his own sister's grave! And *that* is the man who has been calling here on terms of familiarity, making himself quite one of the family! It is a thoroughly good thing that he has left Mansfield, and I, for one, hope that he never comes back to pollute it."

Susan found herself so exasperated by this that, as before, she was obliged to leave the room to prevent herself making some angry remark. Julia's story was so petty, so trifling, so plainly governed by nothing but malice that nobody in their right mind could pay serious heed to it.—Very likely Henry Crawford had encountered Maria Bertram, Maria Ravenshaw as she now was, by pure accident; if she were staying in the neighbourhood there was nothing more likely than that she might have been crossing the churchyard, seen him, or the newly dug grave, and stopped to offer her condolences. What could be more natural, more probable?

And yet, Susan could not help admitting to herself that the story made her uneasy.—She could hardly have said why. She had no reason not to trust Henry Crawford; yet the story made her uneasy.

She was glad that Mr. Crawford had left Mansfield, that she would not be seeing him for some time; she was glad that she had an unlimited period in which to consider his proposal and her own reactions to it.

Would I ever be quite sure of him? she asked herself. A story like that—how trivial. And yet it makes me uneasy. Such a suspicion, in time, would cast a poison on our relations. The poison would be in me, not in him; yet it would be there.

Meanwhile, to her surprise, she began to be aware that Tom's silence and air of constraint towards herself were not prompted by resentment or bad feeling or disgust at her explosive outcry; on the contrary, by small attentions and glances, by the expression in his eyes as he looked at her, she grew to believe that he was profoundly sorry for what had occurred; that he was even wishful to apologise.

In the end he did so, one evening after Lady Bertram had fallen asleep over the cribbage-board and Susan was softly putting away the cards. Tom, with a whisper, summoned her to the other end of the room.

"Susan, I have been mustering up my courage these five days past to say that I am sorry for what I did about Crawford. I should not have approached him in the way that I did. I should not have been interfering in your affairs. It is what I cannot stand in Julia, and it was very bad in me to have done it. If it had not been for Julia and my mother, indeed, I would never have entertained the idea. I should not have heeded them."

Susan, who had guessed as much long ago, did not find that Julia's instrumentality made her feel any better about the incident; rather the contrary; but she said kindly,

"Never mind it, Tom! It was a mistake. We all make them. But it has done no lasting harm. I do not think I should have accepted his offer, in any case. It has given me more time to think it over."

Tom's rather shamefaced look turned to quick inquiry.

"Crawford *did* offer, then?"

"I do not think I am under any obligation to tell you—but, yes: he has made me an offer. I am going to take some time in considering it."

"Susan!" cried Tom; astonishing her, and, very possibly, himself also, "Susan! *Don't* take Crawford! Marry me—do, *do* think of marrying me, Susan! I do not see how we could go on without you, indeed I do not!"

He looked so humble, so beseeching, so uncertain of himself, that Susan was quite amazed. Quickly she said,

"I am very sorry, Tom. I am *truly* sorry. But I cannot marry you—never, never—not just in order to look after Mansfield, you know. I am afraid that is wholly, *wholly* out of the question."

Incautiously, they had raised their voices, he in agitation, she in emphatic repudiation—and Lady Bertram stirred, opened her eyes, and said thickly,

"I was not asleep. What o'clock is it? Is it time for bed already?"

Susan was glad to go to her aunt's help in untangling the embroidery silks from around her slippers; and Tom dejectedly flung out of the room, shutting the door with an emphatic slam. Susan, having escorted Lady Bertram upstairs, retired to her own chamber with a heavy heart. She looked at the two letters, which lay in a filigree box on her table: Fanny's, and that of Henry Crawford. She read neither of them. Instead, she went sorrowfully to bed, but found it almost impossible to sleep.

The following day was a very unhappy one. Susan, looking at the calendar, saw that it was now three weeks since Mary Crawford's death; only three weeks, yet so much seemed to have happened. The world of Mansfield seemed utterly changed. Tom wandered about silent and despondent, or took himself off to the Parsonage; Henry Crawford was gone, and must be missed; and there were no more visits to the White House.

Susan, picking late roses in the garden with little Mary while Lady Bertram drowsed on the terrace, was delighted to see Mrs. Osborne walking across the park, and went out to meet her.

"So! Miss Price, your sister returns in a fortnight from now. You must be very happy at the thought."

"Very, *very* happy," said Susan with truth. "I am counting the days."

"Yet it is a sad prospect for us at the Parsonage," said Mrs. Osborne cheerfully. "A case of 'Hieronymo, 'tis time for thee to trudge.' We shall be under the sad necessity of quitting Mansfield. A parish does not need two parsons, and your brother will most capably fill the office; and his parishioners will be glad to welcome him back."

"But it is very sad that you must go," Susan said sincerely. "Could you not remove into—into the White House? You have become such friends of all of us, you and your brother."

"No, my dear. That would not do. I must return to my own little wilderness in Cumberland, and discover how my poor neighbours have been managing without me. To tell the truth, I have been feeling remorseful about them for some time; many of them are old and poor, very poor, and I find means to be of use to them. I have neglected them for too long. I was eager to come to Mansfield—partly out of curiosity, I must confess—but now it is time for me to leave."

"Curiosity, ma'am?"

"I had heard such a deal about the place from your aunt Mrs. Norris—about you all—that I seized on the chance to come with my brother, having a great wish to see you all in the flesh, to see how the reality measured up to the report."

"And how *did* it measure up?" asked Susan, smiling. "Remembering my aunt, I can imagine some highly prejudiced reporting!"

"Yes; but I was able to sort out the grain from the chaff. And the reality, I must say, has been exceedingly engrossing. I shall have plenty to think about, in the snowy Cumberland winters!"

"Can you not remain, even for a short period, to make the better acquaintance of Fanny and Edmund? And so that Mr. Wadham can have his excavation after the harvest at Stanby Cross?"

"Poor Frank! I fear he will never have the chance to unearth those ruins! He will have to content himself with excavating some Hindoo temple.—No, my dear; we would both find residence in the White

House too sad, after our close connection with dear Mary. Frank was a little in love with her, you know."

"I think that everybody was," said Susan. "She was—she was so uncommon. Different from other people."

"You must not be belittling yourself, my dear," said Mrs. Osborne, looking at Susan shrewdly. "Frank has been a little in love with you too. Frank is very susceptible to beautiful young ladies."

"With me?" Susan was astounded. "Mr. Wadham has always been the height of kindness and friendliness, but surely—"

"Oh, he would never make a push to try and gain your hand, my dear. We have talked it over, very often. He knows that is quite out of the question. We both see that you can never transplant from Mansfield. You and your cousin are made for one another. And Frank would not be so culpably inconsiderate as to suggest removing you to the dangers of a tropical climate, where he has almost died himself. He is, indeed, resigned to dying a bachelor; in fact (between ourselves) I think a bachelor life suits him excellently well."

Susan was so thunderstruck at these revelations that she could only gaze at Mrs. Osborne in silence for a moment or two. Then, after some hesitation, she said doubtingly, "Just now, ma'am, you said—I think I understood you to say—something about my cousin? My cousin Tom?"

"Has he not offered for you yet? Silly fellow! He loves you so dearly—he has been worrying at me for ever about you—wondering if you would have him—wondering how he could bear it if you would not—"

"But, ma'am—don't you think that he wishes to offer for me—simply so that I shall *not* marry Mr. Crawford? Simply so that I shall continue to look after his mother?"

"No, I do not!" said Mrs. Osborne emphatically. "Otherwise I would not advise you to accept him—even if that meant leaving poor Lady Bertram to the tender mercies of Miss Yates!"

"But you do—do you advise me to accept him, then, ma'am?"

"Foolish girl! If I were in your shoes, I would have said *Yes* at the very first opportunity!"

Susan thought of Fanny's letter.

> My dearest Susan:
>
> I confess I am a little alarmed at the thought of your proximity to Henry Crawford. I can see how *that* may develop! You are just the woman for him. And, in many ways, it would be an excellent match, if, as I collect, he has now settled down.

Yes, thought Susan, if I were *ever* quite sure that I could trust him. As I could trust Tom.

> But if you were to marry Henry Crawford, what of poor Tom? It has for so long been Edmund's and my deepest wish that you and Tom should be married. You seem so admirably suited to one another—when Tom has had time to look around him and discover your worth! Pray, pray, dearest Susan, do not do anything *hasty*. Wait, at least, until Edmund and I are at home to advise you!
>
> Your loving sister, Fanny.

"Excuse me a moment, ma'am—" said Susan. "I see that my aunt is just waking up. Do you step up on to the terrace; she will be so delighted to see you . . ."

On winged feet, she herself flew in the opposite direction. She knew where Tom was, in the paddock, doggedly schooling Pharaoh.

Leaning on the fence, Susan called to him: "Tom! Tom! Pray can you come here a moment? I have something I wish to say to you . . ."

What did Susan say to Tom? No more than she should; no more than a well-brought-up young lady may do in such a situation, but enough to inform him that, in the light of further information received from Mrs. Osborne, she was prepared to listen again to his solicitations; to listen with a softer heart and a greater inclination to receive such offers as he might chuse to repeat.

"But how is this, Susan? I thought you had said you would never, never have me?"

This question was asked only after promises were safely exchanged, and her hand in his.

"Oh, Tom! Dunderhead! Had you ever said that you loved me? Not one word! Not one single word on *that*. All you said was—that my aunt needed her companion, and Mansfield its stewardess."

"Well, I am no hand at making fine speeches," said he. "And never shall be, I daresay. But I do love you, Susan—very truly. When I thought I had lost you to Crawford—then my eyes were opened, indeed. I realised all that would be gone from my life."

"Like the dog in the manger that sees its bone taken away," said Susan, laughing.

"Oh, I was in such despair! For three days I thought the sun would never rise again. I thought you were bound to accept him in the end, you know—elegant, clever, accomplished as he is."

"Almost as much so as his sister," said Susan, venturing, with some hardihood, on dangerous ground.

"You know, Susan, that I was half in love with her? I can, I must admit this to you—there must be no secrets between us. She was so very—extraordinary—we shall never meet with her like again—how could I help but love her? You do not blame me for that?"

"Of course I do not, Tom. I fully understand. I loved her, too."

"I knew that I could never—nothing could ever have come of my love. I knew that, almost as soon as I knew that she was dying. We were too far removed from one another's spheres. But she has done me an infinite amount of good, Susan; opened my eyes to so many things that I had never understood previously."

Susan did not make inquiry as to what these things might be. She remembered her friend saying, "Some female unknown to me will in future have cause to thank me."

I have not betrayed my promise to Mary, she thought, for no promise was ever exacted. Thoughtful, perceptive Mary! She knew better than to lay binding injunctions on her friends. Susan must, in course, grieve for Henry, left wholly alone, but she could hope that in time he would find solace; he was an intelligent man, with abilities and resources; he must ultimately be able to find a means to allay grief and worthily occupy his life.

"But do you really love me, Susan?"

"Oh Tom! Blind Tom! Since the age of fourteen, I daresay! Only, of course, I found no difficulty whatsoever in concealing the fact—

even from myself—particularly when you were so overbearing and disdainful and used to address me as *Miss Bones.*"

"I can never have called you that!"

"Come," she said, slipping her arm within his, "let us go and break the news to your mother and Mrs. Osborne."

The marriage of two persons so closely connected, so well suited to one another as Tom Bertram and Susan Price could cause little stir. To the hearts of their intimate friends it gave delight indeed. To Fanny and Edmund, back from Antigua, joyful to be at home once more, the news could only round off their perfect happiness. In Lady Bertram, assured now that she need never be subjected to the fatiguing process of learning to understand the speech and ways of an unknown daughter-in-law, the union of her son with his cousin must induce a deep, if calm, gratification.

"I am very pleased, Susan," she said. "You and Tom had better have the Tapestry Chamber. Mrs. Whittemore will know where the tapestries have been stored, I daresay. And I shall have my garnets cleaned, and you shall have them."

To Julia, of course, the announcement brought unmitigated chagrin. Not only was her despised cousin Susan, the poor relation, the interloper, now put in complete possession of Mansfield Park, able to rule it as she chose, with full right to defend herself against any interference; but also Julia must begin all over again in her pursuit of a husband for her sister-in-law, whose peevish and supercilious ways had by now rendered her odious to the whole Yates household. Her brother had never liked her; and Julia had only tolerated her in the belief that she would be speedily married to Tom and thus established as vicarious authority at Mansfield.

Julia's comments were bitter.

"It was a disgraceful, hole-and-corner business, indeed! But what could you expect, when you introduce vulgar, scheming upstarts into a respectable and honourable establishment? Mansfield is now lost to us for ever. We shall never be welcome there *now.*"

So it proved. Julia's visits became less and less frequent and presently ceased altogether; and, an elder brother of John Yates's subsequently dying and advancing him one step nearer to the peerage, it was found convenient for the family to remove from Mansfield to a dower house where they might keep closer watch over their interest; and so Northamptonshire saw the last of them.

Mr. Wadham and his sister remained for the weddings of Tom and Susan, William and Louisa Harley, which were celebrated at the same time; and then Frank Wadham set sail for the East Indies and Elinor returned to her cottage in Cumberland.

"But I shall come and visit you every summer," she said. "You have not seen the last of me. For it was I, after all, who was the means of uniting you; without my intervention, there is no saying *where* you might be now."

About the Author

The late Joan Aiken was a scholar and a prolific author of children's books and Jane Austen sequels and continuations. She is the author of *Emma Watson,* which completes Jane Austen's posthumously published fragment *The Watsons,* and of *Eliza's Daughter,* a sequel to *Sense and Sensibility.*